IN
COLD
BLOOD

ALSO BY MARK DAWSON

MARK DAWSON

IN COLD BLOOD

A BEATRIX ROSE THRILLER

THOMAS & MERCER

Published by Thomas & Mercer, Seattle

www.apub.com

Amazon, the Amazon logo, and Thomas & Mercer are trademarks of Amazon.com, Inc., or its affiliates.

ISBN-13: 978-1503944237
ISBN-10: 1503944239

Cover design by Lisa Horton

Printed in the United States of America

To Mrs D, FD and SD

Chapter One

The medina in Marrakech was the perfect place if you wanted to disappear. The Red City was a confusing, hectic, mesmeric collection of souks, connected by alleys and passageways that were arranged in no order easy for a foreigner to discern. The busier parts were thronged with a seething horde of humanity, and the central market square, Jemma el-Fnaa, was the busiest. There were youngsters with chained Barbary apes, water sellers in traditional garb with leather water bags and brass cups, storytellers regaling crowds of locals with tales in Berber and Arabic, and snake charmers enticing cobras from small wicker baskets.

The cobbles of the square radiated the baking heat. Beatrix Rose made her way through the crowds, more watchful than any of the others. Her caution was hardwired from a past life that she would never be able to entirely dismiss.

She stopped at one of the many stalls laden with oranges and asked for a glass of juice. It was fresh, cold and strong enough to wash away the bitter metallic taste in her mouth that was a side effect of the medication she was taking. She asked the young stall holder for a refill to take with her and paid him.

He would usually have charged more. She looked like a tourist, after all. Blonde hair, white teeth. Tall and slender. She would have been considered beautiful in any culture. American, perhaps. There were plenty of them around here. But the boy wasn't stupid and he realised that Beatrix was not a tourist. Her Arabic was excellent, for a start. She was tanned a deep brown rather than the florid red that he had come to expect from naïve travellers who underestimated the ferocity of the Saharan sun, and there was a cool knowingness about her that told him that it would have been foolish to try and fleece her. A hardness in her eyes, too, that said trying it would be something he would quickly come to regret.

He was right.

She bought the groceries they needed, then some silver wrapping paper and tape, and walked across the square.

She had an appointment to keep.

She needed to buy a very particular birthday present.

The Café de Paris was one of the hotspots in the chaotic hullabaloo. It was a three-storey establishment with every square inch dedicated to extorting money from the gullible tourists who flocked to it for an authentic local experience. Tables spilled out beyond its curtilage and crammed the interior so that it was almost impossible to move. The third floor was a little quieter, and a balcony with an ornate balustrade offered a beautiful view across the stalls and the mass of people all the way to the Koutoubia mosque and the mountains beyond.

She ordered a mint tea and waited.

After ten minutes, the man she knew as Abdullah sat down opposite her. He was in his early sixties, obese, and the thick-lensed glasses that he wore had the unsettling effect of magnifying his porcine eyes. He was dressed in the garish style of a man who has unlimited funds, but no taste.

"*As-salam alaykom,*" he said.

"*Wa alykom As-salom,*" she replied, returning the greeting.

She looked across the room. A burly man in an ill-fitting suit was at the stairs. His jacket was too tight and it revealed the bulge of a pistol beneath his armpit.

Fair enough, Beatrix thought. Par for the course for a transaction like this.

"Did you get them?" she asked.

"Of course, my dear."

He had a small leather satchel in his lap, the kind that could be had in the souk for thirty dollars, and he handed it across the table to her. She opened it and looked inside. At the bottom was a small package wrapped in oilcloth. She unwrapped it, making sure that no one could see what was inside. There were four suppressors: a .22 Silencero Osprey, a .45 AAC TiRANT, a DeGroat Multi-Calibre and a Thunderbeast 30P-1. They were visually similar, thin tubes that screwed on to the threaded barrels of the handguns. Beatrix owned a varied collection of guns with different calibres, and she wanted to ensure as wide a coverage as possible.

"How much do I owe you?"

"The .45 was a little more difficult to find."

"How much?" she said impatiently.

"Two thousand."

He was taking advantage of her. She doubted whether he had paid more than five hundred. It didn't matter. She had plenty of money, and she knew where to pick her battles. This, certainly, was not the place. She took the money from her bag and passed it across the table.

He reached greedily for it, and as he did, she placed her hand atop his.

The guard flinched and reached into his jacket.

Beatrix ignored him. "Two thousand is extortionate, Abdullah, but I'm going to pay it because I need more from you. And these things will be harder to find."

She was staring right at him, her preternaturally blue eyes icy and cold. The effect of her stare had startled him, as it had startled dozens of men before him. There was no pity in her face. No empathy or understanding.

"What do you need?" he said.

She released his hand, took the list from her pocket and pushed it across the table. He opened it and read, his eyes widening.

"That's a lot of gear, my dear. Are you trying to overthrow the government?"

"Can you get it?"

"I believe so, but not quickly. When do you need it?"

"A week," she said.

"That is possible. It will not be cheap."

"You surprise me. How much?"

He flicked his fingers at the list. "For all this? Ten thousand."

"Fine," she said, getting up. "Get it sorted."

Chapter Two

The sunset was vivid and beautiful, lusty reds and purples and the silhouette of the jagged peaks of the mighty Atlas range. The stall holders lit their flares and the sixty-watt bulbs that they strung from lines that festooned the stalls. The sound of music and excited chatter was everywhere, as was the smell of cooked cheap meat.

A Berber woman stepped into Beatrix's path and offered to decorate her hands with henna. Tourists would often pause and the woman would take out her brush and start to paint, and then scream blue murder when the gullible mark refused to pay the extortionate fee. Beatrix brushed the woman off, and she shrank back into the crowd again.

She had a second appointment to keep.

Johnny's Ink was the best tattoo parlour in Marrakech. It wasn't easy to find, just a small collection of rooms at the back of a building with a shop on the ground floor and a brothel above it. It relied on its reputation. If you wanted quality, you made the effort to find it. The proprietor was American. He was tall and well built, and the ink on his own arms identified him as an ex-Marine.

Beatrix went inside. Orbital was playing loudly on the salon's sound system.

"Beatrix," Johnny said with a warm smile.

"Hello, Johnny."

"How are you?"

"Getting by."

"You want a beer?"

"Sure."

There was a small fridge on the counter. He opened it, took out two bottles of Budweiser, popped the lids and gave one to her.

"Cheers," he said. They touched bottles.

"Have you finished the design?"

"Here." He reached beneath the counter and handed her the outline of the tattoo that he had drawn. She admired it. The design was of a rose. The petals were blood red, deep and vivid. It was beautiful, and exactly what she wanted.

"What do you think?" he asked.

"Perfect."

"Still want to get it done?"

"Definitely."

"Alright. Go and get yourself ready. I'll be through in a minute."

There was another room leading off the reception. She went through. It was stifling and close. She opened the window to let the hot desert air blow into the room.

Beatrix peeled off her top and stood in front of the full-length mirror.

She turned to the right and then to the left, looking at the tattoos that she had already had done in Hong Kong during the long years of her exile. Her daughter's name, Isabella, was written on her right arm, starting at the shoulder and running down to her elbow in elegant, flowing cursive script. On the other side of her torso, beneath her left armpit and halfway down towards the waistband of her jeans, were eight solid blocks of ink.

Each block represented one of the years that she and Isabella had been apart.

The tattoos brought back bitter memories. Getting them done had become her own sad New Year's Eve ritual: she would get blind drunk in a Kowloon bar and find her way to the parlour. The artist, a sweet Chinese girl whose name she couldn't remember, would carefully inscribe another notch in the design.

Beatrix had made sure to leave enough space for more blocks of ink.

She had not expected to see Isabella again.

But she had been wrong about that.

She sat down on the leather couch and waited for Johnny.

He arranged his needles and tubes and placed them into the machine. He collected ink caps, distilled water, his green soap and a bottle of Vaseline. He took a bottle of rubbing alcohol and swabbed her left forearm from the shoulder all the way down to the wrist. He took a disposable razor and shaved away all the fine hair, and then he cleaned the skin with alcohol again so that it was smooth for the transfer. He moistened the skin with stick deodorant and wrapped the stencil around the top of her arm, from bicep to tricep. When he pulled it away, a ghostly purple image of the rose stem and bloom had been left behind. He slathered ointment over it and took up the gun.

"Ready?"

"Do it."

He reached over and punched play on the iPad he had routed through a pair of Bose speakers. Metallica's "Master of Puppets" began to play.

"Here we go."

Mark Dawson

The pain was nothing. Beatrix closed her eyes as the needle started to peck and scratch, and she remembered back to the snow and ice and the numbing temperature of the Russian winter.

A year ago, but it already seemed like longer.

Oliver Spenser had been the first of them. He had tried to run, but Beatrix's knives were faster. She had thrown one into his leg and cut him down, his face ploughing through the drift as the leg went out from beneath him. He had tried to surrender. John Milton would have allowed that, too, but he didn't have the same history with Spenser that she did. He hadn't been tormented by the same nightmares, every night for eight years, so bad that the only way she had been able to silence them had been to lose herself in drink and then, when that had stopped working, the sweet oblivion of the opium pipe. Spenser had begged her forgiveness and then he had begged her for his life.

He must have known that would be futile.

She had sliced his throat from ear to ear and watched his blood pour onto the virgin snow.

One down.

Five to go.

Johnny made an appreciative noise. The linework was done. Beatrix looked down and saw the outline of the petals. "This is going to look very nice," he said as he took out the magnums he would use for the colour. "You still think you'll get the whole sleeve done?"

"Yes," she said. "Leave room for more."

8

Chapter Three

Six thousand miles away, the weather in the Gulf of Aden had been kind. The sea had been placid, the lack of wind rendering it as smooth as a boating lake for the first seven days out of Salalah. Captain Joe Thomas went through the steps of his evening routine. He walked the length of the ship, starting with the port side and ending up to starboard. His main concerns were leaks and dings that he couldn't explain, but given where they were in the world, he also needed to satisfy himself that the ship's security measures were adequate. She was equipped with pirate cages, welded steel bars that fitted over the ladders that offered access from the main deck to the superstructure and then the bridge. The cages were all locked.

It was the third time that Joe had been given command of the *M.V. Carolina*. They had cast off from Oman and were carrying a freight of new cars and trucks to Mombasa, Kenya. She had been built in Russia over fifteen years ago, and she was showing her age in places here and there: the discoloured paint, sticky windows that didn't open, pieces of equipment that were often temperamental. She was six hundred feet long and ninety feet abeam, painted orange on the hull and white on the superstructure, and she had two forty-foot cranes positioned fore and aft. Her top speed was nineteen knots, and she was propelled by an enormous diesel engine. She was a big ship, a leviathan, with enough capacity to carry more than a thousand of the containers that would be hauled on the landward legs of their journeys by eighteen-wheeler rigs. They had been assigned the run that stopped in Djibouti in the Republic of Djibouti and then at Mombasa, Kenya, on the Indian Ocean.

He stopped off on the bridge to say goodnight and then climbed down into the accommodation area. They called it "the House." It was a six-storey superstructure positioned at the stern of the ship, and it had everything that the crew needed to meet their minimum human requirements: their living quarters, the mess and the hospital. At the top of the structure was the bridge. It was functional and far from luxurious, but Joe had seen worse facilities during his thirty-year career.

He stopped in the mess hall. The off-duty crew were gathered at the dinner table, most of them working their way through a meal of burgers, fries and bottled water.

Joe took an empty seat and looked around the table at his crew. The chief mate was on the bridge and would stay there all night. The chief engineer, a doughty Virginian called Nelson, was joking with the third mate, the chief steward and the bosun. There were a total of twenty able seamen aboard, and six of them were in the mess room tonight.

Another group of four men sat at the second table, picking idly and disinterestedly at their fries. He had briefly introduced himself to them when they had come aboard, as he was making his final checks, but he had had no contact with them since then. They were obviously not sailors and seemed to prefer to keep to themselves. They tended to eat alone, and they didn't socialise with the crew. They were big men, well built, with hard faces, and they all had short cropped haircuts. The epidemic of piracy centred around Somali waters had finally persuaded the executives back at HQ that it made sense to provide their ships with armed guards. These four were ex-soldiers from a private security outfit called Manage Risk.

Joe went over to them.

"Evening, gentlemen," Joe said. "We haven't had a chance to speak properly yet."

The men looked across at him with surly dispassion. "Evening," the nearest one said.

He remembered their names from the crew manifest.

Joshua Joyce.

Paddy McGuinness.

Rafe Bloom.

Lee Anderton.

But that was all that he knew.

"Which one is Joyce?"

"Me."

"You're in charge?"

"That's right."

"Good to meet you."

Joyce shrugged.

"How are you finding it?"

"It's fine."

"First time aboard?"

"I've been to sea before," he said tersely. "Just not for as long as this."

The crewmen were listening. "Was the sea like this?" the steward interrupted. "Trust me, fella, this couldn't be easier."

Joyce didn't reply, but Joe could see that he and the others didn't share that opinion. He could understand it. It wasn't sea sickness. That would have passed by now, and the *Carolina* was so big that even decent swells would mean just a slight thud beneath the feet when the bottom of the ship hit. No. It was tedium. The crew had a hundred things to occupy them every minute of every day. There was a routine to follow, and he had always found that to be an effective way to stave off the boredom and the loneliness of a long voyage. And for the crew, at least for most of them, this was a vocation. They were born to be on the sea, and the monotony of the long days and the long nights were part of what made it what it was. These men were not sailors. They were military. They had nothing to do except check their weapons, keep up to date with the latest intel and watch whichever crappy films the men had donated to the ship's library.

"I'm glad you're here," Joe said. He took out a folded printout and laid it on the table. "Just got this."

"What is it?"

"We get a regular email from the Office of Naval Intelligence in Maryland. They give us a heads-up of what we might need to look out for. You know we're going into dangerous waters now, right?"

"Yes."

"They're reporting even more activity in the area than usual."

Joyce read it. "Forty-five attacks?"

"And that's just in the last week. That's a new record as far as I can tell."

The other men quietened down.

"Forty-five?" Nelson said querulously.

"Forty-five." Joe raised his voice so that everyone could hear. It wouldn't do any harm for them to know what they were sailing into. Keep them on their mettle. "A Danish ship was attacked yesterday. The *Danica White*. Sea was too rough and they got away. But it was close. They got a grapple up."

"Where?"

"South. Not far south, though."

If Joyce and his men were concerned, they didn't show it. "It's nothing to worry about."

Nelson turned around so that he could see Joyce properly. "You ever been run at by Somali pirates?"

"I've had plenty worse than that."

"You reckon? I don't know. I was on a ship last year. Chemical tanker, Japanese—the *Golden Nori*. We had three skiffs come at us. They followed us for two days and then made their move. We sank one of them with the water cannon, and the other one broke down, but the third one, man, I'm telling you, that motherfucker kept coming on no matter what we did. They got their boarding ladders up the side, almost got them latched on, but we managed to fire a flare at them and set them on fire. It was a lucky shot. Nine times out of ten, it misses. And if it had missed, they would've boarded us."

"What's your point?"

"My point is I've seen what those boys are like. They ain't scared of nothing. Nothing."

"Did you have guards on board?"

"No."

"You do now. And we've got plenty of gear with us. We'll shoot them out of the water if they're stupid enough to have a go. We won't need lucky shots with flares."

Braggadocio? Maybe. "Glad to have you aboard, fellas," Joe said. "Let's hope it doesn't come to that."

———

He scarfed down a burger, found his way to his quarters on E Deck and slumped down onto his bed. He was all done in. He had been up since six, and there had been one thing after another, so much so that he had hardly stopped. No use moaning about it, he chided

13

himself. It comes with the territory. You make it to captain of a ship like this, and you take the added responsibility that comes with it.

Didn't mean he couldn't be dog tired.

He took off his shoes and socks and lay with his back propped up against the bulkhead. He grabbed his laptop and fired it up. The screensaver was one of his favourite pictures: him, his wife Sheila and both his kids, Maisie and Richard, in the back garden of his mother-in-law's house. It was a hot summer day during his last shore leave. He'd had six weeks off and he had squeezed every last drop out of it. Trips to see Richard's t-ball team and Maisie's violin recital, a short holiday in Maine, pizza night on Friday and trips to the movies on Sunday. It had been heaven, and it had been even harder than usual to pack and go away. That was just the way of it.

Six weeks off, six weeks on. Being a merchant mariner wasn't like a normal job. Even anti-social jobs, like those where you had to work nights, you could still get to see your kids. It wasn't the same for Joe. When he was working, he was thousands and thousands of miles away from the people he cared about most of all. Reading stories to the kids over Skype had been fun for a while, but it had paled. Eventually, it had just highlighted what a poor substitute it was.

He opened his email and drafted a quick message to Sheila. She knew that this route was a little more dangerous than others, but she had been married to him for long enough so that he didn't sugar-coat his updates to her. He told her that they were just running past the coast of Somalia and that he would be glad when they were out of the way. Some captains had been detouring a hundred miles to the east to put decent distance between them and the coast, but that added days to the journey, and Joe was nothing if not punctual. He was a professional. Hitting his deadlines meant something to him. Sheila knew that. He signed off and pressed

"Send," and then spent twenty minutes surfing the net until his mind stopped racing.

He undressed and got into the narrow cot. He was asleep almost as soon as his head hit the pillow.

Chapter Four

Beatrix headed north, making her way out of the square and into the network of roads and alleyways around it. The road was narrow between the shoulders of dilapidated buildings on either side, and people fought for space with scooters and bikes that darted in and out of gaps. Taxis nudged impatiently up at those in the way, and small motorised delivery carts whined along on two-stroke engines. It was prayer time and the mournful cries of the muezzins rang out from the speakers fixed to the tower of the nearby mosque, an ululation that clashed with the honking of horns and the animated to and fro of outmatched tourists bartering with grizzled traders. The air was freighted with smells: sweat, an array of spices from the market, the richness of leather goods that had cooked in the sun all day. It was a bewildering conflation of noise and motion, and it would have been a disconcerting assault on the senses to those with no experience of it. Beatrix moved through the crowds with the confidence borne of experience. She had been here for a year, and there had been visits before that.

Visits in the furtherance of a profession that she had long since given up.

She moved to the heart of the medina and then took a series of turns that led her deeper into the heart of the Red City. She loved exploring this warren of back streets. Eventually the touristy shops made way for local market stalls selling everything from brass pots and pans to linens, colourful spices, local dresses and delicious food. The presentation was amazing, store owners painstakingly piling the produce as high as it would go. Lining the souks were two-foot-tall containers of spices and bowls of olives infused with herbs. There were antique stores full of dusty artefacts. Occasionally, the lanes opened into courtyards where children kicked footballs, and homeowners returned from a day of fruit and vegetable shopping; mobile sellers peddled past on their bicycles.

Beatrix turned off. A first left led into a narrow alley, the next right into a narrower passage, then another left and she was into an alley so narrow that she could touch the walls on both sides without extending her arms. She passed doorways that led into shops and homes and darkened maws that led into even narrower tunnels that disappeared into darkness. The people were fewer and the sounds diminished. The final right turn would have been easy to miss, a slim passage that was cool and quiet, the surface beneath her sandalled feet uneven and worn. Finally, she stopped at a battered oak door studded with iron rivets, marked with a tiny sign on the jamb: "La Villa des Orangers."

She took the large iron key from her bag, pushed it into the lock and opened it.

Stepping through the door was like stepping back two hundred years. The riad had once been the home of Grand Vizier Madani El Glaoui, and the previous owner had clearly relished its heritage. The door gave onto an open vestibule and then, beyond that, to a beautiful, peaceful space. The riad was three storeys high and set around a quiet and peaceful courtyard that featured four mature orange and lemon trees and, at its centre, a plunge pool of the clearest crystal blue water. The cooling effect of the courtyard was no accident. The courtyard's open roof channelled the warm air that entered the riad, passing it over the pool and cooling it. The cool air then circulated back upwards, lowering the temperature in the rooms. The walls were decorated with *tadelakt* plaster and *zellige* tiles, with quotes from the Quran written out in beautiful Arabic calligraphy.

The sale had been something of an emergency. Beatrix discovered later that there had been a bit of a scandal, and the owner had had to disappear quickly. As a result, he had been forced to leave all of the fittings as well as two original Julian Schnabels, a collection of Andy Warhol prints, African sketches and Berber oils.

The ground floor offered space for the kitchen, dining room and an old-fashioned *hammam,* or Turkish bath; the second and third floors contained six large bedrooms and bathrooms. The roof was open and furnished with sun loungers that were shaded with large parasols. The madness outside was muffled by the thick walls, with the result that the space was a tranquil, calming oasis.

Beatrix hung the key on its hook on the vestibule wall and went through into the courtyard.

"Miss Beatrix," said Mohammed. "How was the square?"

"Just as always," she said, dropping her bag on the floor. "Crazy."

Beatrix had bought the riad when she arrived. She had paid cash, using the money that John Milton had demanded from Control before they both had double-crossed him. She had always known that she would end up back here. She loved the city and the riads that were dotted around it, the stunning juxtaposition of peacefulness and clamour that one could access just by stepping over the threshold and turning a few corners. It was also the perfect city for someone who wanted to be off the grid. It was a simple matter to sink beneath the surface and be absorbed by the madness, and should the circumstances ever demand it, the senseless array of thronged streets would be perfect for losing a pursuer.

Beatrix did not expect to be followed yet, but she had plans that, once set in motion, would mean that her targets would do anything to find her before she found them.

And since they were almost as deadly as she was, it made sense to settle somewhere where she could disappear.

"Did you get what you wanted?" Mohammed asked her.

She indicated the bag. "I did. Where's Isabella?"

"On the roof."

"Good." She took out the roll of silver wrapping paper. "I need some scissors."

The roof was a little higher than those around it. It offered a spectacular view of the city and, in the hazy distance, the dun brown of the desert and the Atlas Mountains that rose up on the horizon. The roofs of the neighbouring properties accommodated air-conditioning units and satellite dishes, a couple of other riads set up much like this one: a series of sun loungers, large parasol umbrellas and low tables.

Isabella was lying on one of the Balinese loungers that Beatrix had bought. She was wearing cut-off denim shorts and a thin shift, and a pair of Beatrix's glasses that were too big for her slender face were propped on her forehead. There was a jug of orange juice and a stack of books on the table next to her.

She hadn't noticed her mother yet, so Beatrix watched the girl for a moment. They had been apart for eight years, and Beatrix had cherished every moment of the year that they had spent together since their reunion. Isabella had been just three years old when she had been taken. The picture that Beatrix carried in the locket around her neck showed her as she was then—small and chubby, with long curls of blonde hair. She had grown up into a beautiful girl. She was slender and tall for her age, with skin so porcelain white that she had to be careful in the sun and hair that had been straightened and lightened, long enough to reach down beyond her shoulders.

Beatrix felt pride and regret when she looked at her: pride because Isabella had turned into a fine young woman and regret because she had missed the incremental changes of that transformation. There had been a series of foster homes and institutions before John Milton had arranged for her to be returned to her grandparents, and then to her mother. When Isabella was in the mood to talk about it with her mother, it was clear that it had not been an enjoyable time. She had not been mistreated, at least as far as Beatrix could divine, but it was a childhood bereft of real love and affection. The girl had retreated into herself and was introspective and insular as a result. It had taken her a little while to be comfortable in Beatrix's presence. She was self-reliant and confident, though, and that was good. Those were traits that would be very useful.

She stepped up from the stairs and made her way across the roof.

"What are you reading?"

"Mummy!" Isabella said, her face breaking into the most guileless smile.

Beatrix stooped and picked up the book that her daughter had laid across her lap. It was a book on Arabic.

"How are you getting on?"

"Good, I think," she said.

"Let's hear it, then."

"*Hello, how are you? My name is Isabella Rose.*" She said it haltingly, her accent still a little rough.

"Not bad," Beatrix replied. "You're getting better."

Beatrix poured two glasses of orange juice and gave one to Isabella. The girl drank hers quickly.

"I have something for you," Beatrix said.

She handed her the wrapped present and sat on the edge of one of the loungers as Isabella tore the paper away. She pulled out the four thin metal tubes and held them up for inspection with a delighted grin.

"Suppressors?"

"That's right."

"Why are they different?"

"They each fit different guns."

"I didn't realise they'd be so simple."

"It's a simple idea. It just muffles the sound the expanding gas makes when you fire the gun. Like a balloon. If you pop it, it's loud, right? But if you untie the end and let the air out . . ."

"It's quiet."

"Exactly. Quieter, but not silent. They still make a noise."

"I love them."

She smiled as she watched her daughter turning the suppressors between her fingers. "Happy birthday, baby doll. Thirteen today."

"Can I try them?"

"Of course."

They went down the stairs to the courtyard. The north wall was given over to a long, thin room that might once have been used to stable horses. It was dark and a little cold after the heat on the roof. Beatrix took a shawl and wrapped it around her daughter's shoulders. The room was twenty feet from wall to wall; at the far end was a target that had been affixed to a container filled with sand.

She took a 9mm Glock from its hook and carefully screwed the Osprey onto the threaded barrel.

"Okay," she said. "Take me through the drill."

"Do I have to?" the girl protested.

"You do."

"You know I can do it. I just want to shoot."

"Handling the gun safely is just as important," she chided. "You always need to know when it's loaded and when it's empty. And what would you do if it jammed?"

"Okay." Isabella gave up the argument.

"What would happen?"

"I'd be in trouble."

"No, you'd be dead." She waved a hand. "Go on, then. Do it."

The girl took the gun and, with her finger outside the trigger guard and the gun aimed away from them both, pushed the release button and pulled out the magazine. She racked the slide three times to make sure there were no rounds in the chamber. She pulled the slide back again and used the slide lock to hold it in place, then checked again that the chamber was clear.

It took her less than five seconds.

"Weapon is clear."

"Good," she said. "Now load it."

She took a box of 9mm full metal jackets and pressed ten of them, one after the other, into the magazine. She shoved the magazine into the well with the heel of her palm and showed it to her mother.

Six seconds.

"Good. Now fire it."

Isabella pushed the slide release button, popping a round into the chamber. She settled into her stance, wrapping her fingers around the handle with her thumbs pressed together on the left hand side of the gun. The gun looked oversized in her small hands.

She fired ten times, her shoulders absorbing the recoil and the suppressor dulling the sound of the report. When she was finished, she removed the magazine and looked into the breech to make sure that it was empty. She handed the gun to her mother and walked quickly down the range to look at the target.

Beatrix was pleased, but not surprised: all ten bullets had found the two innermost quadrants. "Well done," she said. "Very good."

"It's much quieter."

"Much," Beatrix said. She was pleased. The noise of the unsuppressed firearms was too loud for her to be comfortable firing them on the range. Even in a noisy city like this, it would only have been a while before someone had started to ask questions. Now, though, Isabella would be able to practise as much as she wanted.

"Can I go again?"

"Yes," Beatrix said.

She took the gun again as Beatrix noticed Mohammed standing at the open doorway.

"Too loud?" she asked.

"Not at all. Very quiet, in fact."

"What is it?"

"There's someone here to see you."

"Who?"

"His name is Michael Pope. He says you'll know who he is."

Pope?

"Where is he?"

"Waiting outside. Shall I tell him you're not in?"

"No," she said. "Show him in. Show him up to the roof, please. I'll be right there."

Beatrix felt nervous.

"Who is it, Mother?"

"Someone I've wanted to see for weeks."

"Is it about them?"

"I hope so. Go to your room, please, Bella. I'll tell you what he says when we've finished."

Isabella ejected the magazine, racked open the slide to remove the chambered round, then put the gun and the ammunition away in the cabinet.

Beatrix felt excited, too.

It was starting.

Chapter Five

The telephone woke Joe Thomas up. It seemed as if he had only just closed his eyes, but as he fumbled for his glasses, he saw that it was five-thirty in the morning. He looked at the porthole window and saw that dawn had broken.

"What is it?"

"You better come up here, Captain."

His first thought was of pirates. It was the right time for it. Just after dawn and just before dusk were the haziest times of day in the Gulf of Aden, and visibility dropped down to around three or four miles. They were the best times for a skiff to make an approach. It could be almost right on top of you before you knew anything about it.

Joe got out of bed, jogged down the central corridor and then climbed the chimney, ascending the ladder to get to the bridge. It was a wide space, with large windows that ran from the ceiling to waist height, letting in plenty of light and allowing excellent visibility in every direction.

Vasquez, his chief mate; Harry Torres, the second mate; and another able-bodied seaman called Mike were keeping watch.

Joe went over to the conning station, a console filled with navigation aids. To port was a chart table where Torres concentrated on gathering all the information that they needed to run the ship safely. He had access to the Global Maritime Distress and Safety System, which furnished them with weather updates, and a small electronic station from where he could send and receive radio messages.

"What is it, Ray?"

"We've got something," Vasquez reported.

Joe looked at the radar. It was a small screen, like a television or a computer monitor, with objects appearing as small blips. Additional data were provided alongside the main image, including the speed of any of the vessels and the estimated time when their courses would intersect.

He saw two small white dots. They were four miles behind to their starboard quarter and coming at them quickly.

"How fast are they?" he said, more to himself than to the rest of the men on the bridge.

"Fast," Vasquez replied.

"Radar estimates twenty knots," said Torres.

"Do the security boys know?"

"They say they're getting ready."

"Weather report?"

Torres shook his head. "Like this all day."

It was calm and serene. Bad weather would have helped them, but they weren't going to strike lucky today.

Joe took up his glasses and scanned the sea until he saw a bow wave, the wake one of the boats was kicking up as it chopped through the water.

Another blip appeared on the radar. This one was behind the first two, and it was larger.

"The mother ship. Vectors say he's trailing us."

The radio crackled.

"Somali pirate to freighter. Somali pirate to freighter. Respond."

"They tried to call us five minutes ago."

"Did you answer?"

"No."

Joe looked at the radio. The Somalis were broadcasting on the International Hail and Distress Channel.

"Somali pirate to American freighter. We have you. We are coming to board."

Vasquez's voice was taut with tension. "Why are they telling us? Don't they want to surprise us?"

Joe took up the glasses again and swivelled through three hundred and sixty degrees, scanning all four quadrants. He saw another bow wave to the north, and then, as he turned to the south, he saw another.

"It's a trick. Misdirection. They've got four skiffs and a mother ship. They're coming at us from three different directions."

The skiff to port was the closest and therefore the most immediate threat. He focused the glasses on it: it was painted red, ten metres long, with a big outboard engine. The wake stretched out behind it, a frothing trail through the green-blue waters. Too far away to make out its crew yet. He checked the radar: it was three miles away, closing quickly, and would intercept them in five minutes.

"Seaman," Joe said, "go and see where security is set up. They need to know we've got multiple targets coming in three different directions: port, starboard and astern. Make sure the cages are shut, double-check them, then distribute the flares."

"Aye." The able seaman, an Aussie called Ryan, left the bridge.

"Increase revs to one hundred and fifteen."

Torres was in control of the engine order telegraph. "One hundred and fifteen revs," he called out in confirmation.

"Call UKMTO and tell them we're about to be attacked."

UKMTO was the United Kingdom Maritime Trade Operations. They handled security in the Persian Gulf and Indian Ocean. Vasquez made the call and gave them their coordinates, together with the threat they believed they were facing, the number of boats and the answers to the other questions they had.

"Change course to one hundred and ninety degrees."

"One ninety," the helmsman said. The quartermaster repeated the order and swung the wheel.

The ship began to turn.

"UKMTO says the nearest warship is a day away," Vasquez said. "We're on our own, Captain."

As soon as he had finished his tactical assessment, Joshua Joyce knew that they were looking at a difficult morning. They had plenty of firepower: American M-14s chambered for .308 rounds and British SA-80s provided most of the arsenal, and he was equipped with a Barrett M107CQ sniper rifle. The problem was manpower. There were only four of them, and that meant that he was going to have to place one man on the stern, one to port and one to starboard, leaving himself on the flying bridge to coordinate. That offered them precious little flexibility. With attacks coming in from three directions, all it would take would be for the pirates to fluke a lucky shot or for a weapon to jam, and a whole flank of this enormous ship would be vulnerable. He would be able to stand in and fill any gaps that developed, but there was no flexibility for them at all. He had thought about involving the crew, but they didn't look all that handy, and he didn't want to risk it unless it was absolutely necessary.

One of the seamen, an Aussie, approached him with a portable radio clutched in his hand. "It's the captain," he said. "Wants to talk to you."

He took the radio. "Captain?"

"You know the situation? Four skiffs coming in, a mother ship staying out of range behind them?"

He put plenty of confidence into his reply. "Yes. We've got it under control."

"I'm going to change course a couple of times and see if I can't make the wake a little choppier for them. That'll make things more difficult for the boats astern, but the two to port and starboard are too far ahead to be affected. They're coming in, whatever we do. I've got men on the hoses. We'll start pumping them when they get into range, but it's touch-and-go whether they'll have much effect. I wouldn't bank on it."

"You don't need to," Joyce said as he started to assemble his sniper rifle. "How far out are they?"

"The nearest is two miles out. Closing fast."

"I've got a fifty-cal sniper rifle up here," he said. "Anything within five hundred metres might as well be right next door. Have you seen what a big bullet like that does to a man's head? It's not pretty. I plug a couple of them, they'll lose their lunches. They'll turn around quick."

"You can make a shot like that?"

"Don't worry, Captain," he said. "I'm the best. That's why I'm so expensive."

———————

Joe called down to the engine room and told them they were going to need to squeeze every last rev out of the engines. That would be a delicate balancing act. Too slow, and it would be easy for the skiffs to reel them in. Too fast, and he would blow the gaskets and they would be helpless.

He looked down at the radar. The closest skiff was less than a nautical mile away. They were travelling at seventeen knots. The skiffs were doing twenty.

"Sound the intruder alarm."

The third mate sounded the ship's whistle and then went over and activated the alarm. If anyone was still asleep, they wouldn't be for long. They needed every man at his post.

"Turn on the pumps."

The *Carolina* had powerful pumps positioned all around her. They kicked in and started to send powerful streams of seawater in forty-foot gushes. The pressure was significant, enough to buffet a boat off course or fill it and submerge it if the flow hit it head-on.

"Get the crew to the safe rooms. Lock the engine room."

"Aye, sir."

Joe had been in the Merchant Navy all his life. He had never had reason to fire a gun, nor could he remember ever seeing anyone else fire one in his presence. Nevertheless, he recognised the chatter of an automatic rifle as the guard on the port rail fired a warning volley into the sea ahead of the skiff.

The boat kept coming.

⌣

Joyce watched as the skiff ignored the warning shots. It was his funeral. He raised his glasses and studied the boat coming in towards them from the port side. The *Carolina* was casting out a series of furrowed waves from the bow, but the skiff was able to address them from an angle and bounced across from one to the other. He counted five men aboard, and it looked like they were well used to the sea. They absorbed the impacts as their boat leapt up and slammed back down again, rocking to and fro, without needing to anchor themselves.

He watched with the glasses as the man in the front of the boat raised a rifle and aimed forward. He heard the crack of return fire, bullets ricocheting off the superstructure. The boat was still a good quarter mile away, but if there had been any doubt that they were serious, that had now been allayed. Rounds crashed against the metal housing, and another rang off the smokestack high above his head. The others aimed and started to fire, too. It looked like they had AKs. Not surprising.

"Joyce to Squad," he said into his portable handset. "Shots fired. Repeat, shots fired. Tangos armed with automatics. Weapons free. Weapons free."

The flying bridge was the open space directly above the main bridge. It was one of the highest points on the ship and was a good spot to settle in with a sniper rifle. The M107CQ had been designed for situations where the firepower of a .50 calibre rifle was required but the bulk of the M82 or M107 series was impractical. CQ stood for "Close Quarters," and it was ideally suited for use in helicopters and watercraft. This big ship, steady and unwavering, would offer a pretty solid platform to shoot from.

Joyce brought the rifle around and rested the bi-pod against the safety rail that prevented the drop to the deck below. He pressed the stock into the groove between his shoulder and neck and sighted down the Leupold Mark 4 telescopic sight. He swept the sea until he had the skiff in the sight and then aimed at the man in the bow. Hitting him would be a potent demonstration for the men behind him. He squared the man's head in the reticule, took a deep breath and slowly released it, exhaling to a natural stopping point. He waited until his muscles were calm and he didn't need to inhale, and then he squeezed the trigger with a good, crisp pull.

The .50 calibre round closed the distance to the man before he even heard the deep report of the gun. One moment he was living, the next moment he was not. Joyce absorbed the recoil against his shoulder and kept sighting the target. The round was designed to stop materiel. It made a very big mess of flesh and bone. Snipers called it "pink mist."

He had expected the boat to check its pace, but it did not. The men ducked down a little and the firing paused, but they did not reduce speed. He put the glasses to his eyes again and watched as another of the men crawled to the bow and hauled the body of the headless pirate over the gunwale, tossing him into the wash. The body floated for a moment, spun in the waves and then sank from sight.

They started firing again.

"They're fucking tenacious," radioed Joyce's number two, Paddy McGuinness. He was a gruff Ulsterman, and it took a lot to fluster him.

"Keep firing."

He let the glasses fall on their strap and sighted with the optics again. The boat was two hundred feet away and darted around to make itself more difficult to hit. Joyce changed tack. He sighted the bow and aimed backward, down the boat, until he had a shot at the glossy black outboard motor. He relaxed his shoulders into the shot, breathed in, and fired.

The fifty-calibre bullet streaked out and crashed into the engine, pulverising the casing and ripping a tunnel through the machinery. The boat was near enough for Joyce to hear the engine splutter and then fade out, and as he looked, the boat lost speed and drifted away.

He thumbed the portable radio. "One boat disabled," he reported. "I took one of them out. Had no effect. Go for the outboards."

Joe and the third mate, Barry Miller, sat on the floor, beneath the metal wainscoting that reached up four feet above them. Bullets rang against the metal, bouncing around, ricocheting. Joe figured that they were safe unless there was a crazy rebound, but that didn't make it any less terrifying. The skiff to port had drifted away without its engine and was out of the fight. He crossed the bridge to starboard and looked down. The pirates were a hundred feet away and eating up the distance between them. One of the security men sent a barrage of fire down at them, but he missed, the surface of the water interrupted by a series of small plumes, the boat racing through the spray regardless.

The radio crackled again.

"Captain, you must surrender ship. We have RPGs. If you do not allow us to board, we will fire. We will destroy you, Captain."

Joe toggled the radio. "Joyce. They're saying they've got RPGs. Is that true?"

There was a pause.

"Affirmative."

It was Joe's turn to pause.

Joyce came back again. "Captain? What's your opinion?"

"What range do they have?"

"They're in range now."

Shit, shit, shit. He concentrated on keeping a calm and decisive exterior, but he was floundering. "If they get a grenade into a tank or on the bridge, we're done for. We'll end up drifting, at best.

At worst . . . Good God, it doesn't bear thinking about what could happen. We've got to surrender."

"Negative, Captain. That's not what you're paying us for."

Joe ducked down beneath the wainscoting as the Somalis loosed a barrage at the bridge. A line of bullets studded the superstructure.

"Fifteen degrees left and then fifteen degrees right," Joe called out and the AB yanked the wheel, turning them away from the skiff. It was a delaying tactic, at best.

"Captain," the Somali said over the radio. "Do not resist. We have you."

Joe heard the curse over the radio and then, loud and strident, Joyce barked out, "Incoming! RPG fired, port side."

A projectile arced up from beneath the obstruction of the super-structure and fell in a graceful parabola that ended on the deck. The grenade detonated between two containers, a beautifully contained little explosion that still sent a barrage of shrapnel against the superstructure.

"Incoming!" one of the other guards yelled.

Two more hits, this time at the body of the ship, and the sudden blooms of black smoke unfurled and rolled up the side and across the bridge.

"Captain!" Vasquez yelled. "We're on fire to port."

Joe could see the thick cloud of smoke stretching up over the gunwale and onto the deck.

"Thomas to Joyce," Joe said firmly into the radio. "Stand down. Repeat: stand down. We haven't got a choice. We surrender."

The end of the battle had been quick and bloodless. The pirates had boarded the *Carolina* without difficulty once the shooting had stopped. Each skiff had a long thirty-foot ladder with hooks at one end, and they had simply raised them up so that the hooks fastened down over the six-inch fishguard. They had scaled the ladders and swarmed aboard. Joe had counted twenty of them, and a man had been left in each of the three skiffs that were still operational. The fourth skiff, with the wrecked outboard, had drifted away. The trawler had picked it up once the hijacking had been completed.

Joe opened the channel on the portable radio. "We've been boarded. Repeat: pirates aboard."

He moved quickly. He radioed the first engineer in the engine room and ordered him to take the steering. The men down there would lock themselves inside. It would take hours, perhaps even days, to find them and break through.

The cages did not appear to have detained the pirates for very long. After ten minutes, a thin man, young and with catlike, cunning eyes, entered the bridge. He was armed with an AK-47. Two others came with him. Both of them had semi-automatic pistols. They aimed them at the officers on the bridge.

The thin man spoke first. "Who is captain?" He turned to Vasquez. "You are captain?"

"No, I am," Joe said. "I am the captain. This is my ship."

"Very good."

"We have money. We have a few thousand dollars on board. You can take it."

"This is not about money, Captain. We do not want it."

The words didn't process. Joe continued, following the script that he had prepared. "My employer will not pay a ransom."

"You do not listen, Captain. We do not want money." He indicated with the AK that Joe should step away from the console. "My name is Farax. I am in charge here." His broad gesture might have meant the other men, but it was not lost on Joe that it encompassed the bridge and the rest of the ship, too. "What is your name?"

"Name's Joe Thomas."

"You are American, Joe?"

"That's right. Boston."

"That is good. And how many men do you have on board, Joe?"

"Just ten of us," he said.

Farax smiled. "I know you lie. A ship like this has twenty men. Perhaps thirty. But it does not matter. Ten is enough. You will tell them to come here."

Joe still did not understand, although a dim, recessed part of his brain had started to stitch things together. He refused to acknowledge it, though. It was too horrible to consider.

"I can't do that."

"What do you mean?"

"The men are around the ship. They have important jobs to do. They cannot leave their stations."

"You must call them, Captain. I do not ask you again."

Joe shrugged that he couldn't help.

Farax raised the muzzle of the AK and pointed it at Ray Vasquez's chest. "I do not ask three times," he said as he pulled the trigger.

The machine gun was horribly loud in the confined space of the bridge. The rounds studded Vasquez in the chest, and he staggered back against the console, a look of incomprehension on his face as he slowly slid down until he was resting on his backside.

"I am not a pirate, Joe. I do not want money. I am al-Shabaab. Do you understand what I mean?"

Joe didn't have the ability to speak. He nodded.

"Now. Please gather your crew. If you do not, we kill you all now."

Joe looked at him and knew, immediately, that this was not a bluff. What he had done to Vasquez was evidence enough, but more than that it was the way the man looked at him. There was no compassion in the dark orbs of Farax's eyes, no empathy. If he said he would do something, then he would do it.

Joe picked up the radio and keyed it open. "This is the captain," he said. "I'm going to need the officers to report to the bridge. All officers, to the bridge."

They lined the men up against the wall. Joe stood between them and Farax. He didn't know what he would be able to do. Perhaps he might be able to talk him down, reduce the temperature. The thing that worried him more than anything else was that Farax did not appear flustered or perturbed. He smiled at the other pirates, conversing with them in easy Arabic, and his posture was loose and relaxed. It was as if what he had just done was of no consequence to him whatsoever.

The other officers arrived. They were all scared. Joe was scared, too.

The soldiers were the last to arrive. Joyce wore a black expression, but, like Farax, he moved with an easy step. Joe guessed that this was not the first time he had looked down the barrel of an AK-47. The other men—McGuinness, Bloom and Anderton—had a similar demeanour.

"That's all of us," Joe said.

Farax looked them over. He walked over to Joyce. The difference in physique was striking: Joyce was tall and powerful, and the Somali was slender.

"My name is Farax," he said. "What is yours?"

"Joyce."

"And what do you do on the ship, Joyce?"

"I'm the chef."

"You do not look like a chef."

Joyce shrugged. For a moment Joe wondered whether he was going to say something they might all regret, but he held his tongue.

Farax had to look up a little to look into his eyes, but he did, and held his gaze. It was Joyce who looked away. The Somalis evidently found this amusing.

"You go to our ladder now," Farax said. "We go for journey together."

Chapter Six

Captain Michael Pope was standing at the raised wall, looking out over the city. He was a tall man, well built, and it wasn't difficult to tell that he had a history in the armed forces. He was dressed conservatively, in beige chinos and a blue poplin shirt. Beatrix cleared her throat, and he turned around to face her, removing the sunglasses and hooking them into his shirt pocket.

"Number One," he said.

"No," she said. "Not any more. Not for years."

"Rose, then."

"It's alright. It's Beatrix."

"Beatrix it is."

He smiled. Michael Pope had been in post ever since Control, the man Pope had replaced, had fled the country. Beatrix and John Milton had destroyed half of the Group in Russia and served notice that they were coming for Control next. Beatrix knew Milton better than she knew Pope, but the things that she did know about him suggested that he had been a very fine soldier and that he would make an excellent commanding officer of the off-the-books death squad of which she had latterly been the prime operative.

"How are you?"

"I'm good."

He waved an arm at the view. "Nice place you have here."

She brushed it off with wry disdain. "All thanks to the government's money."

"How much did you get out of them?"

"Two million dollars."

He shook his head in amused satisfaction. "The least they could do after what Control did."

"Yes, it was. But his debt is nowhere near paid."

"No," he said. "I know it's not."

"Is that why you're here?"

"Not about him—not yet."

"So?"

"It's about the others. One of them in particular."

She motioned for him to sit and followed him across the roof. On cue, Mohammed climbed the stairs with a platter that held a silver pot of sweet-smelling tea. Mint tea was central to Marrakech culture, and he took special pride in his old family recipe. There was a spearmint plant in the courtyard, and he stripped handfuls of leaves from it every morning; the leaves, sugar and a good tablespoon of gunpowder green tea would have been added to boiling water and left to steep before he brought it upstairs.

"Miss Beatrix?" he said as he approached.

"Do you want some green tea?" she asked Pope.

"Please."

Mohammed set the glasses down and poured the tea from a height so that a thin layer of foam settled on the top.

"Thank you," Pope said.

Mohammed ducked his head; he looked at Beatrix, and she gave a slight, barely perceptible nod. He carried one of her Glocks in a holster beneath his *djellaba*, and, had she shaken her head, he would have taken it out and shot Pope there and then.

"Is there anything else, Miss Beatrix?"

"No, Mohammed. That's all. Thank you."

With a watchful look back at them, he smiled thinly and went to light the candles in the lanterns that were set around the roof. When that was done, he went back downstairs. Beatrix knew he would be waiting just below.

"Who's he?" Pope asked.

"An old friend," she said, and that was true. She had worked with him on an assignment ten years earlier when he was a corporal in the Moroccan Royal Guard. She had saved his life, and it was to him that she had gone when she'd moved here after leaving Hong Kong. She had asked him if he could recommend anyone to run the house for her and had been flattered when he had insisted that he would do it himself. He was a good man, and she trusted him implicitly.

Pope sipped his tea and replaced it on the table.

"How is your daughter?"

"She's well."

"How has it been—the, well, you know—the time?"

"Since I saw her? It's been difficult."

He spoke carefully. "Does she remember what happened?"

Beatrix tightened her grip on the glass a little. "She remembers me. I haven't pressed her on the rest, but I think she does. I don't know how you could forget something like that, no matter how young you were."

Watching your father shot in the head.

Your mother shot in the shoulder.

Your mother stabbing a woman in the throat.

"No," he said, seemingly uncomfortable with the subject he had raised.

41

She had no time for his awkwardness. "It's been a year, Pope."

"They don't want to be found, Beatrix. And they know how to hide."

She had no time for excuses. "What have you got?"

"I'm not sure you'll like it." She gave a terse gesture that he should continue. "None of them are going to be easy to find—you know that—but we've located Joyce. He's had an interesting career since he left the Group. He worked as a mercenary for the first few years—Iraq, Afghanistan, all the usual places. That seemed to get old for him, so he switched to private security instead. There's a company based in North Carolina called Manage Risk. Branches all over the world, hundreds of ex-forces men. They have contracts for all kinds of things, including nautical security. They get paid by the big shipping companies to sit on their freighters so they can put up a fight if pirates attack."

"So he's in America?"

"It would be a lot easier if he was. Look at this."

He handed her a copy of the *Times* from the previous day. The above-the-fold article on the front page reported upon the hijacking of the crew of a freighter off the coast of Somalia. "What about it?"

"He was aboard."

"Security?"

"Yes. The Somalis have put skiffs out all the way up and down the coast and they've been trying their arm with the big freighters. It's like pilot fish trying to take down a whale, but something must have gone wrong with the guards on this one. They got on board somehow. We don't have any intel on that yet."

"What do you know?"

"That they took the crew back to Somalia."

"Where?"

"We don't know. They're still at sea. They're being tracked, though. We'll know when they make land."

"That's good."

"Good? How?"

"Because when they do land, I'll know where Joyce is."

He smiled patiently. "He won't be there for long."

She was incredulous. "They're not going to pay the ransom?"

"No. The ship has Americans on board: the captain, a few of the officers. It's not the first time this has happened, and the government has had enough. These boys are al-Shabaab . Very militant al Qaeda. Salafist jihadism, strict sharia, all that. They make bin Laden look like a choirboy. There's no possible way that the Americans can be seen to be dealing with them, so the administration has decided it's time to make an example out of them. They're going to send in the SEALs who got bin Laden to get the hostages back and take the pirates out."

"When?"

"It won't be long. They'll find out where they are and plan off that. I'd guess three days, but they're not keeping us in the loop. We have our sources, of course . . ."

Beatrix was already planning how it might go down. Somalia was all the way on the other side of the continent from Marrakech. It would take a week to drive. That was obviously going to be too long. Could she fly? She could get a charter flight to somewhere nearer and then drive the rest of the way . . .

"Beatrix," Pope said, interrupting her line of thought. "Please tell me you're not thinking about going to Somalia?"

"If that's where he is, that's where I'm going. It's been a year and that's the first lead you've found for me. I can't afford to let him get away."

"Let the Americans get him out. We'll track him afterwards."

"What if he dies in the raid?"

"Then he's dead. Move on to the next one."

"No. It has to be at my hand. I'm going to be the last person he sees."

Pope protested. "The SEALs are very good, Beatrix. They'll break him out, and he'll go back to wherever it is he's been hiding. Only now, we'll know. I understand why you want to be the one who pulls the trigger, but if you get yourself killed, the others will get away with what they did. You've got to pick your moment. This isn't it."

"You don't think I can do it?"

"I didn't say that, but this is a big risk."

"Thank you, Pope. You've been very helpful."

"Would anything I say make any difference?"

"No."

Because I don't have forever to find them.

———

Beatrix warmed a little to Pope as the evening drew in and, eventually, she decided to invite him to stay for dinner. She would benefit from a better relationship with him, and so far, his cooperation had been won by threats as much as anything else. She still retained copies of the evidence of his predecessor's duplicity, and she had threatened to release it if he did not offer his assistance in tracking down the agents who had been at her house that particular afternoon. The four surviving agents plus the man who had sent them after her.

He accepted her invitation and they moved to the dining room. It was painted a deep chocolate with dusky blue velvets and was lit by three large candle lanterns. The ceiling was painted with a mural of the desert's midnight sky, and the furniture was handmade from dark wood. Beatrix and Pope had gin and tonic, and Isabella, when she eventually joined them, had a large glass of orange juice.

"You must be Isabella?" Pope said as she sat down.

She looked at him shyly.

"Isabella," Beatrix said. "Mr Pope is working with me. Say hello to him."

"Hello," she said bashfully.

Mohammed's wife, Fatima, worked in the riad as their cook, and she prepared a tajine, bringing the conical earthenware pot to the table and serving it in front of them. They had chicken served with olives, preserved lemons, parsley and saffron, and it was, as Pope confirmed after clearing his plate and a generous second serving, delicious.

Isabella had a glass of mint tea with them and then went up to her room as the two of them enjoyed glasses of wine.

"Have you heard from Milton?" she asked him quietly.

"No," he said. "But I don't really expect to."

"You don't know where he went?"

"No. And I'm not going to try and find him if he doesn't want to be found. He's been running long enough."

Pope took out a packet of cigarettes and offered her one. She took it and pushed across one of the Lalique ashtrays that had come with the place when she bought it.

"Look," he said. "What about Joyce?"

Her tone became colder. "What about him?"

"Are you really serious about going to get him?"

"I don't joke about things like that."

"Then at least let me help you."

"I'm all ears."

"How are you thinking of getting there?"

"I haven't really decided yet."

"Surely you have to fly?"

"I know. I was thinking about getting a charter to Kenya."

"You can't take weapons on a charter."

"I'll find them at the other end. Have you been to Somalia before, Pope?"

45

"No. But you have?"

"Once."

"Where?"

"Mogadishu."

"What for?"

"You remember President Farrah?"

Pope nodded. Farrah was a warlord who had declared himself president of Somalia in 1995. "I know he caused plenty of problems."

"Until he got shot."

"That's right, I remember. He died of a heart attack on the operating table."

Beatrix smiled. "That's what they said." She made a syringe with her thumb and forefingers and mimed the plunger being depressed.

He looked surprised. "Seriously?"

She shrugged. "That's what I heard."

"Well, I'll be. I didn't know that."

"Believe me, Pope, if Somalia is anything like it was then, it won't be hard to find an AK."

"But wouldn't you rather have your own?" He swept an arm out in the direction of the courtyard. "I'm taking it you have some here."

"Of course I do. And yes, I would. But I'll do what I have to do. If I have to be flexible, that's fine."

"Look—how about this? The RAF flew me in today. It wouldn't be such a big deal to divert on the way home. I'm sure someone back in London could come up with a reason why we need to stop off in Kenya on the way home. That way, you can bring your own gear with you. I might be able to arrange transport for you at the other end, too. At least it will get you to the border."

"If you could, that would be helpful. But you'll have to be quick. I'm going tomorrow."

"No, that's fine. I'll make a call tonight. I don't think it'll be a problem."

He sipped his wine, and again, his face betrayed his unease.

"What is it?"

"What about Isabella?"

"She'll stay here. Mohammed and Fatima live here, too. They'll keep an eye on her."

"I didn't mean that," he floundered. "What about if—"

"If I don't come back? I am coming back, Pope."

"But if you didn't—"

"—then she would manage very well. She's lived most of her life without me. That was one thing Control taught her—how to be self-reliant."

The conversation was a little stilted after that. Of course, the possibility that Beatrix might be robbed of the scant time she had left with Isabella had crossed her mind. It wasn't as if she had an indeterminate amount with which to play. Each minute was precious, but it needed to be balanced against the desire for vengeance that she had fostered during her exile. She had nurtured that from a spark to a blaze, and now there could be no possibility of extinguishing it before she ran out of time. There was more to it than her own satisfaction. Once she started on the path she had chosen, Isabella would be in danger. Once she started to eliminate her targets, she had to assume that the others would realise what was happening and the danger that they were in. They would retaliate—she knew that she would, if the roles were reversed—and they would know that Isabella had already proven to be a valuable disincentive to violence on the part of her mother. They would come for Beatrix, and if they couldn't find her, they would come for Isabella instead.

Pope was looking troubled. "Wouldn't it be better to just . . ."

"Let bygones be bygones? Would you do that, if you were me?"

"I don't know. Maybe. If I had as much to lose."

"Then we are going to have to agree that we're just different people. I have my reasons. Revenge is just one of them."

He ran his finger around the rim of the empty glass. "I respect that. And I promised that I'd help you. I'll stick to that promise."

"Thank you," she said.

He put the glass back down on the table. "It's late. I should be going."

"You're welcome to stay," she said. "We've got more guest rooms than we know what to do with."

"Are you sure?"

"Of course. Mohammed will show you up."

"What about you?"

Thinking of her targets had stirred up bloody thoughts. "I've got things to do," she said.

Chapter Seven

The Somalis were using an old trawler as the mother ship. They had transferred the six officers plus the four soldiers from the *Carolina* to one of the skiffs, sailed south for three or four miles—Joe couldn't be sure—and met up with the trawler when the big freighter was just a smudge on the horizon. The ship was in a terrible state, barely seaworthy, and for the first time that day, Joe had been grateful that the surface of the ocean was glassy smooth. The four skiffs, including the disabled one, had been tied to the back, and the trawler had towed them behind it as they set sail to the west. The pirates had lined up Joe and his men on the deck, five abreast, with two Somalis guarding them with AK-47s. The sun was now directly overhead and blisteringly hot. They had been given a two-litre bottle of water to share out between them, and Joe insisted it be rationed carefully. He did not know how far they had to go.

As it turned out, they sailed for ten hours before they saw land. It appeared as a dark line on the horizon, and then, as they drew closer, details began to emerge. They were headed for a town. Joe looked at it as they rose and fell on the swells. There was a thin outcrop of rock that protected the littoral, an old Portuguese lighthouse standing uselessly at the westernmost tip. Behind the natural harbour wall was a port, with skiffs tethered to wooden jetties, and a fringe of beautiful white sand that would have graced the pages of the most exclusive holiday brochure curled away around the rim of the bay. Beyond that was the town, a series of square white buildings in the familiar Somali fashion. Behind the buildings was desert, everything coloured with burnt reds and oranges.

Joyce was sitting next to him. His team had thrown their weapons over the side when it was obvious that they were outgunned. That made sense.

"Do we know where that is?" Joyce asked him.

"We've been heading southwest," Joe said. "There are a few coastal towns like that all the way down to Mogadishu. Hobyo, Haradeere, Barawe. I don't know enough about them to know which one it might be."

"You ever been here before?" Joyce said.

"You kidding me? No."

"I have."

"What the hell for?"

"Old job," he said vaguely.

"And?"

"What's it like? You don't want to know. The worst place on Earth. The very worst place."

The Somalis said very little. Farax had the best English. The others spoke it in a rudimentary fashion, just enough to make themselves understood.

There was plenty of time for thinking, and Joe had spent it trying to work out what was happening to them. Normal procedure would have been to stay on board the ship until the ransom had been delivered, usually dropped from a plane to land on the deck. And normally, the ransom would have been paid. What was twenty or thirty million dollars compared to the value of the cargo, the ship, the crew? But Farax said that he was not interested in money, and nothing he had done since had suggested that was untrue. The alternative was unpleasant, and Joe did everything he could to avoid thinking about it until he could not avoid it any longer. He knew about al-Shabaab from the newspapers and the television. Somalia had been torn asunder by a brutal civil war that had raged without cessation since the late eighties. The fighting had made it a failed state, a place with no effective government, and into the vacuum had come the terrorists who thrived in lawlessness. Al Qaeda had based their camps here. They had been replaced by al-Shabaab, "the Party of the Youth," who had seized whole towns and held them. Joe didn't know much more than that, apart from the fact that the commentators he had read agreed on one thing: they were worse than al Qaeda.

Much worse.

Farax had been sitting at the stern of the boat for most of the journey. The skipper had reduced their speed as they approached the coast, and now they were drawing to a standstill. A sea anchor was dropped over the side. Joe watched the young man as he pushed himself upright, stretched his arms, gathered his AK and stepped carefully until he was in front of him. He lowered himself to his haunches and pointed to the town ahead of them.

"That is Barawe," he said. "Do you know it, Joe?"

"I've heard of it."

"Al-Shabaab controls it. It is our town. Look at it."

There was a crystal-clear lagoon and, beyond that, rows of white houses, square and boxy.

"You will stay here with us."

"For how long?"

"For as long as it takes for our message to be heard."

"What message?"

"Our message of jihad. Your government must listen, Captain. You will make them listen."

Joe bit the inside of his mouth, unwilling to press for fear of the answers that Farax might provide. He looked at the man: he was young, in his mid-twenties if Joe had to guess. His skin was clear, his eyes were large, the whites prominent against his very dark skin. He was absently stroking the tips of his fingers against the barrel of his battered old AK.

"You answer question for me, Joe," he said.

"If I can."

"You have man with long rifle aboard," he said, unable to find the word for *sniper*. "He shoot man and then shoot engine, yes?"

Joe shook his head. "I don't know what you mean."

"Big gun. Fifty calibre."

Joe felt Joyce stiffen next to him.

He shrugged at the question.

"You must tell me who did this."

"I'm sorry, Farax. We have no one like that."

Farax smiled at him again, the same smile that he had used just before he had pumped half a dozen rounds into Vasquez's chest, but this time there was no repeat. "I understand why you say nothing. I do the same, if it were me. But I know you have men here, on boat, who are soldiers. Sailors do not use such weapons. They do not have the skill. And a soldier is worth more to al-Shabaab than a sailor. You must remember that, Joe. You understand?"

"I do, but it's not relevant . . ."

Farax laid a hand on Joe's shoulder. "We will talk about this again."

The Somalis untethered the skiffs and brought them around the port and starboard. Farax indicated that they should get into the boats, and once they were safely aboard, the sixty-horsepower outboards were opened all the way to maximum, and they bounced across the shallow waves into the harbour. It was a wet, bumpy ride, and Joe held on to the gunwale. They swerved into the opening of the harbour, flashed past the abandoned lighthouse and proceeded to the shore, driving right up the beach. They lurched to a sudden stop. One of the other hijackers shouted at them, "Out! Out!" and they did as they were told. Joe's feet slapped down onto the wet sand as the second and third skiffs followed them up the beach. Joe looked around and saw a fleet of small boats on the beach, attended to by twenty or thirty men. Some were working with angle grinders and welders on engine mountings; others were siphoning fuel, while others were attending to damaged hulls. The area was busy with activity. Whatever this place was, it was important to them.

They were led at gunpoint up from the harbour, through dusty streets, the sun's glare blindingly bright against the whitewashed walls. The foreigners were penned in by the Somalis, who walked with AKs lowered and readied. There was no use in trying to resist—where were they going to go? Local fighters appeared along the street as the procession climbed up from the beach, and soon there was an excited, fractious atmosphere. A couple of the men from the boat aimed their AKs into the air and fired off celebratory rounds. It set off others, and soon their passage was marked by an ear-splitting barrage.

Joyce was alongside Joe, who had watched as he had been herded from the trawler. The man's *sangfroid* was remarkable. On first glance he might have appeared to be above it all, but Joe had watched him carefully, noticing that Joyce was observing everything and everyone, soaking it all in. The signs of stress were difficult to find. There was a barely noticeable tic in his right cheek, above the line of his jaw, but that was it. Joe knew next to nothing about him or the men from Manage Risk. He had been pleased that they had been included on the crew roster but, save that they were all ex-military, he was ignorant about them.

"You can't give us up," he told Joyce in a terse whisper as they climbed natural steps to the street level above.

"I wasn't about to."

"They will kill us if you do. You know that, right?"

"I won't say anything."

"And your crew?"

"They're good men. They won't either."

"What he was saying about soldiers, that was true. This is all about propaganda. If they think we're all just sailors, maybe we get out of this in one piece. It'll definitely give us more time."

"You don't think this is about a ransom?"

"These boys? No. They don't need money. They run the coastline north of here. They don't need whatever it is your company would pay to get us back. This is about ideology. We are their chance to make a big splash."

"So . . . what will they do?"

"They'll hold us. Parade us in front of the cameras. Get us to make statements denouncing the Great Satan, all that shit. I figure we've got six months before they change tactics. It might get dangerous then, but that's more than enough time for your government or my employer to decide to teach these pricks a lesson they'll never forget."

Joe looked up, eyes forward, and saw that Farax was watching them. His eyes glittered with malevolent interest, cunning, and Joe suddenly felt as if the young man had the ability to look right through him. He swallowed down his fear as they continued on.

They headed north. They passed a mishmash of construction styles: the boxy white houses, concrete blockwork buildings with corrugated tin roofs, dwellings that were little more than tents. There were a handful of shops with little in the way of goods on display. There were no bars and no sign of any alcohol anywhere. People continued to stop and stare at the incongruous little parade.

The man in the lead stopped and pointed sharply to his left. They turned through a gateway not even big enough for a car and into a reasonably large compound. It was walled on all sides by an eight-foot rendered barrier that, while crumbling in places, would still be a significant obstacle to scale for anyone who might come and rescue them. There was a brushwood hut in the corner of the yard where two goats bleated at the disturbance. Steel gates slammed shut behind them, sealing them inside.

The house in the middle of the compound was three storeys high. It was made from thick stone blocks, and the windows were thin and miserly, covered by green shutters. The entrance had once been grand, but the fine design had been blasted by the salty wind and no one had cared to maintain it. The house was topped with a decorative crenulated pediment that had also been scarred by the passage of time, and when they got closer, Joe saw jagged holes where the stone had been chipped away by automatic gunfire.

There were two armed guards at the main door, and they moved aside as the procession approached. They went inside. It was dark and damp and difficult to make out any details. They passed drums of well water, a hole-in-the-floor privy and a series of rooms in which bedrolls had been arranged. Quarters for the men, Joe guessed. They continued deeper inside; the leader paused at a door to unlock it and then opened it to reveal a flight of stairs that descended to a basement.

"Down," he said.

They did as they were told. There was a single bare light bulb at the foot of the stairs, and in its feeble light, the descent on the stone treads, slick with moss and lichen, was treacherous. There was a further door at the foot of the stairs, and it, too, needed to be unlocked.

"Here. You stay here."

Joe was the first inside. It was a large room that must have stretched out beneath the footprint of the house above, with dimensions of perhaps twenty metres by ten metres. There was a rough dirt floor, concreted over in places, damp from moisture that streamed from the ceiling and ran down the walls. It was windowless and lit only by the dull light that seeped in through a grid of ventilation bricks set into the wall just below the ceiling and by another bare sixty-watt bulb, not nearly bright enough to dispel the deep shadows in the corners of the room. A tarpaulin had been spread across a quarter of the space, and a series of mattresses had been stacked atop it. That was their sleeping arrangement. There were no chairs. A couple of buckets on the far side of the room were the toilet facilities.

"We can't stay here!" Harry Torres exclaimed.

"What would you prefer?" Farax asked him.

"I wouldn't keep my dog down here."

"Harry," Joe said. "Take it easy. That won't help."

"Come on, Joe, this is bullshit."

"And getting agitated about it is not going to help us at all. Calm down."

Torres flashed a hot stare at him, but held his tongue.

Farax retreated to the door. "I will return later, Joe," he said. "Perhaps we can talk about improving your accommodation. You know what you have to do."

Joe's stomach turned over. He could feel Joyce's eyes in his back. "I'm sorry, Farax. Really."

"Later, Joe. We talk later."

The door shut behind him.

Chapter Eight

Mohammed showed Pope to one of the guest rooms. Beatrix went back down to the shooting range and unlocked both cupboards. She collected her gear into a pile on the floor: a pair of Kiowa lightweight tactical boots, Mechanix fingerless gloves, a Tactical riggers belt and a collection of magazine and dump pouches. She added night vision binoculars, a Leatherman Wave multi-tool, two hydration pouches and a zippered nylon pouch that contained twenty-four anodised steel throwing knives. She dropped in three flash-bangs and three fragmentation grenades. Her primary weapon was a Heckler & Koch MP-5 with a full thirty-round magazine in the weapon and another couple of spares. She chose a Glock 17 for her secondary weapon. Both the Glock and the MP-5 were chambered for 9mm cartridges. She wanted to carry only one type of cartridge.

If she needed anything else, she would scavenge it when she got to Somalia. She knew it would be simple enough to do.

The last item she added was her *kukri*. It was a large, curved knife that was much favoured by the Gurkhas, the Nepalese soldiers with whom Beatrix had served in Iraq. It had belonged to a corporal who had died after Beatrix had rescued another two of his men. They had given it to her as a token of their gratitude. It was a little shorter than her forearm, kept in a leather scabbard that she could fit to her belt, and carried with a steel that was used to repair the edge of the blade.

She packed the gear in a waterproof rucksack and locked the range behind her. It was a bright night with a full moon overhead, and eldritch light flooded down into the courtyard. The square aperture overhead framed the abundant star field like a painting. Beatrix sat by the plunge pool, took off her sandals and dipped her feet into the water. It was icily cold and refreshing, and after just a handful of seconds her skin was tingling and alive. She looked around at the courtyard and then up to the second and third storeys. This was all hers. She loved the city, and she knew that, had circumstances been different, she could have made a good life for herself here. But there was no point in fantasising about that. It was not the hand she had been dealt. She allowed her thoughts to drift, and for a moment, she lost a little of the fierce resolution that had driven her ever since John Milton had persuaded her to come out of hiding and leave Hong Kong behind.

Could she stay here and enjoy the time that she had left? There were eight years to catch up with Isabella. That would be challenging, but it would also be rewarding.

She felt the itch of the tattoo on her arm.

There was space there for five more.

Pope couldn't seriously have expected her to just let it go.

She was owed a debt and she meant to collect it.

A blood debt.

To be paid in full.

Her room was the biggest and most luxurious in the riad. It had its own veranda, swathed with bougainvillaea, overlooking the makeshift roofs and minarets of the city. She enjoyed the view and the cool night air for a moment and then returned to the bedroom. The walls were painted pink, with tiny pieces of glass mosaic embedded within them. There were rustic woollen curtains on the wide windows and a pompom-fringed throw on the bed.

She was tired, but her bones ached, and she knew that she wouldn't be able to sleep. She went into the large bathroom, its walls of polished cream *tadelakt*, and drew a bath. She undressed and slipped into the steaming hot water, where she lathered herself with the orange peel soap and the Argan oil that Mohammed sourced from a supplier in the souk. She had endured eight years of privation during her exile before John Milton had found her. She was prepared to spoil herself now.

There would be precious little time for any of that later.

She untethered her thoughts and let them drift. They travelled back across those eight years, the most recent lost to her amid the intoxicating clouds of sweet opium, all the way back to her flight from England, and then to the events that had forced her to leave.

There had been an operation in London. Group Fifteen had been tasked with eliminating two targets. They were given no information, which was standard operating procedure, but she later discovered that they were supposed to have been dealing contraband weapons to the Syrians. That was the cover story, but it wasn't true. They were Russian agents, and Control, the man Michael Pope had replaced, had been caught like a rat in a trap. He was corrupt, and rather than face the choice of flipping or being burnt, he had ordered them both to be executed. The operation had been Milton's first, and he had frozen. Beatrix herself had killed one of the agents and a Spetsnaz bodyguard, but the other one, a man named Shcherbatov, had escaped. She had retrieved intel from the wreck of the car they had sprayed with bullets and discovered the truth behind the hit. When she confronted Control, he had reacted in the way that cornered rats most often react.

He had attacked.

That memory was especially fresh. She remembered the little details: the crisp day in early autumn; the bright blue sky with scudding clouds; the way the sunlight shone against the red of their freshly painted front door.

The five agents who had been waiting for her in her house.

Number Five: Lydia Chisholm.

Number Eight: Oliver Spenser.

Number Nine: Connor English.

Number Ten: Joshua Joyce.

Number Eleven: Bryan Duffy.

She remembered her husband, Lucas, on the settee in the front room, his arm around a three-year-old Isabella.

Chisholm shot Lucas in the face and managed to put a shot into Beatrix's shoulder before Beatrix had thrust the point of a letter opener into Chisholm's neck.

Beatrix would have killed every last one of them, but they had Isabella. It had been a stalemate: as long as they had her, there was nothing Beatrix could do.

She had escaped the country and stayed away for eight years. Control had ensured that Isabella was swallowed up by the foster system, her name changed, kept hidden from her mother. Milton had forced Control to give her up. Her grandparents had taken her until Beatrix was able to get into the country to be reunited with her.

Now it was a question of settling scores.

How many of them were left?

Was Chisholm dead? That would need to be confirmed.

She had murdered Spenser in the grounds of a dacha in Plyos, north of Moscow. She had drawn a line through his name, etched his rose on her arm.

Three or four of them remained to be dealt with.

Plus Control.

Especially Control.

But Joyce would be next.

Beatrix used her memories. They were her fuel. She looked up at the second floor and the room where her daughter was sleeping as the fire she recognised so well took hold, scorching away her doubts and reservations. Her will was irrelevant. She had no choice. She did not have the luxury of the softer option. If any of those agents found out that she was still alive, they would come for her. They were all peerless killers. Machines that would keep coming and coming and coming until she was dead. They would have the advantage of surprise, and there would be nothing that Beatrix would be able to do to stop them. Isabella would be in the gravest danger, and that was something that she would not permit.

No.

Not again.

She had no choice.

She would invest the time that was necessary to wipe away every single threat that might threaten her precious little girl. She had been absent throughout Isabella's childhood, and making her future safe would be Beatrix's way of making amends.

A mother's gift to her child.

Chapter Nine

Beatrix awoke a little later than normal. She was usually up at five, but it was six now. Her body was preparing itself, perhaps, for the difficult task that was ahead. She showered, sloughing away the torpor of sleep, and then stood in front of the mirror to inspect her reflection. Her life in Hong Kong had been unhealthy, and she had lost a lot of weight and all of the muscle tone that she had gathered over the course of her career. She had worked hard lately to correct that. She had a set of free weights in the range downstairs, and she usually began the day with an hour's worth of exercise. Now, her arms and legs had started to assume their old litheness, and her shoulders were cambered with muscle.

She dressed in a pair of loose black trousers and a plain white T-shirt and went downstairs.

Mohammed brought her a glass of freshly-squeezed orange juice and the international edition of the *Times*.

"Where's Pope?"

"I think he is just rising now."

"And Bella?"

"Gone for a run."

Most mothers would be concerned about that in a place like Marrakech but Beatrix was not afraid at all. Isabella could handle herself.

Beatrix left the newspaper on the tiled table next to the pool and took the orange juice into the range. She looked at the rucksack that she had packed last night, pregnant with weaponry. She opened the armoury, took out another magazine of 9mm rounds and slipped it into the bag. She zipped it up again and hauled it out into the courtyard.

Isabella opened the front door and stepped into the *riad*. She was wearing a T-shirt and shorts and the new Nike running shoes that they had bought together the previous week. She was sweating lightly, fronds of her blonde hair stuck to her forehead.

"Hello, Mum."

"Good run?"

"Five miles. It's getting easier."

"Then do ten."

She looked at the rucksack next to the pool. "Where are you going?"

She sat down next to her daughter. "I have to make a quick trip."

Isabella was a tough child—her peripatetic childhood had guaranteed that—and she had become skilled at hiding her emotions. But she was unable to disguise the panic that crossed her face. "How long for?"

"Just a few days."

"You're coming back?"

"Of course I'm coming back."

"Promise?"

"I promise, Bella."

She looked at the rucksack again. She knew very well what must be inside. "Have you found one of them?"

"I have. That's what Mr Pope came to tell me."

"Who?"

"Joyce."

"Where is he?"

"In Somalia. I'm flying to Kenya with Mr Pope, then I'm going to drive across the border."

"And you're going to kill him?"

Beatrix nodded.

"Good," Isabella said.

"Mohammed and Fatima will be here with you."

"I'll be okay."

"I know you will, but I want you to listen to them and do what they say. Do you understand?" Isabella nodded. "And I want you to keep training. You can shoot as much as you want to now. Mohammed will help you if you have any problems. You need to work on your accuracy. By the time I get back, I want you to be putting one out of every three shots into the middle of the target. And next week, we'll make it one out of every two."

"When can I try the automatics?"

"When I get back, baby doll." She smiled. "They're noisy. We'll need to go out into the desert for that."

Isabella nodded, swallowed down sudden emotion, and stepped into Beatrix's embrace. She buried her face in her mother's shoulder, snuffling a little. Beatrix cupped her hand around the back of the child's neck and held her there for a moment. She saw Pope descending the steps from his room on the second floor, and she disengaged, kissing Isabella on the top of her head and stepping away.

"I love you," she said quietly.

"I love you, too."

Mohammed carried her rucksack through the alleyways to the street where he had parked the car, and loaded it into the back. Pope had already left for the airport to make the arrangements. Beatrix told him she would meet him there later. Beatrix got into the car, and Mohammed drove them through the town to the Palmeraie, the expensive enclave on the northern outskirts of the town. The surgery overlooked the immaculate greens of the Palmeraie Golf Palace, banks of sprinklers cascading water onto them in a display that Beatrix found rather excessive and vulgar.

Beatrix had been able to afford a private doctor. The luxuriously appointed reception was an exercise in expensive minimalism: frosted glass, leather Eames sofas and soft classical music piped through hidden speakers. There was an internal fountain, the water tinkling musically, and tasteful prints were hung from the walls. Everything was designed to distract those who were rich enough from the worry of their ailments. The other waiting patients were arrayed around the room, reading magazines and drinking tea that was brought to them by a deferential member of the staff. It reminded Beatrix of a hotel or a spa. She found it difficult to stomach in contrast to the squalor just a few feet from its doors, the penniless sick who would die from their poverty as much as from their illnesses. She would never have chosen to come here, but she had the money and there was no alternative. She could not sacrifice Isabella and the pursuit of her future safety for the sake of her scruples.

The receptionist announced softly that the doctor would see her, and she followed the familiar corridor around to his open door. His name was Abdeslam Lévy. He drove a Porsche Cayenne, lived in a big villa on the outskirts of the city and was putting his three children through an expensive private education. Beatrix had researched him very carefully. Old habits died hard.

"Beatrix," Lévy said in the manner of someone greeting an old friend. "How are you feeling?"

"Not bad," she said.

"Given the circumstances."

"Of course."

"You've been taking the morphine?"

"Every day."

"And it's helping?"

"Yes," she said. "The pain is better."

"Very good. That's about as good as we could have hoped for."

"Given the circumstances?"

"Yes." He smiled in what she took to be a paternal fashion. "You've come to talk about the scan results?"

"That and something else," she said.

"Well, let's talk about the scan first, shall we?"

She nodded; she didn't really care about that since all it would do was recalibrate the time she had left and, therefore, the time she had to accomplish the tasks that she had set herself. Useful enough, but it wasn't going to change the conclusion they had already reached.

"It's good news," Lévy said. "The tumours in your lungs haven't grown. If anything, they might even have receded a little. And so that's good. The Docetaxel is working as well as we hoped it would."

"What does it mean? Practically."

"It means we have it under control for now. We'll do another scan in a couple of weeks, but if it keeps inhibiting growth, we might be looking at the higher side of the average I gave to you."

"So, a year?"

"Yes," he said. "Maybe a little more. As I said, it's good news."

A year. *Yes,* she thought, *that was good news.* The initial prognosis had been bleaker than that. She had found the tumour while she was in Hong Kong: a tiny pea that she could almost roll between her fingers when she showered. She had known, of course, that she should have had it checked out, but she had been wary of anything that would record her details, especially her DNA, on any kind of online database. She knew, from experience, how quickly something like that would have been picked up by the people who were looking for her, and so, initially, she had done nothing and felt it grow a little each day.

By the time that she had paid a rogue doctor to examine her, the tumours had spread: dark shadows in her lungs and spots in her liver. Surgery was pointless by that stage, and so she had the first of two courses of chemotherapy, both of which she had administered herself in her dingy room. There had been two more courses since, both in the peaceful treatment room off Lévy's office with the view of the garden and the colourful birds that visited it.

Lévy's treatment had been more successful.

The doctor was looking at her expectantly. "You said there was something you wanted?"

"Yes. It's about the morphine. I'm running out. I need the prescription refilled."

He frowned and scrolled through her records. "Really? You should have enough left for the rest of the month."

"I don't."

"You've been taking one a day?"

"Yes," she lied.

"Then I don't understand. I prescribed you two months' worth five weeks ago."

"There must have been a mistake." She shrugged. "I've run out."

She looked at him expectantly, aware of how unnerving her crystal blue eyes could be. Lévy looked back, couldn't hold her gaze, looked down at her records, looked back at her and then, defeated, printed out a new prescription. "This is two weeks' worth," he said. "One a day, no more. The last thing we want is for you to overdose. If you think you need to increase the amount, you'll need to discuss it with me. Understand?"

"Of course," she said, taking the script and folding it neatly. She put it in her pocket. "Thank you."

"Is there anything else?"

"Yes," she said. "We had an appointment in the diary for next Monday. I'm going to have to postpone it."

"That's fine. Just tell Mobina on the way out." She stood up. "Good luck, Beatrix," he said.

Beatrix didn't have much time for luck, but she took his hand when he offered it, smiled, because that was what he expected, and went back outside. She handed the script over at the pharmacy window and pocketed the white bottle that the chemist brought back. She went outside. It was a bright, warm morning, and she stopped in the pleasant garden that faced the surgery.

Mohammed was waiting in the car, parked on the road a hundred feet away.

"How was it?"

"It's not getting any worse."

"So? How long does he think?"

"Maybe a year."

"You will have time to do what you want to do, then."

"That depends on what Joyce tells me or what Pope can find out."

"Yes. But you will have more time with Isabella. To finish her training."

"I will," she said.

The pain in her bones flared again. She cracked open the bottle and tipped two of the little blue pills out onto her palm. She dry swallowed them, put her Oakleys on and settled back as Mohammed put the car into gear and drove them away.

Chapter Ten

Joe woke to the sound of the town slowly stirring. He could hear the two goats in the yard complaining, the sound of children playing in the streets nearby and cockerels welcoming the new day. He had slept badly. The mattress was uncomfortable, and even when he had been able to sleep, he had been plagued by nightmares. He knew that Joyce was right. This wasn't a commercial deal. It was political. He had heard about the things that the Islamists did to their prisoners, the things that they did in order to get YouTube clicks and prominence on news reports.

He sat up. Most of the crew were either asleep or lying awake on mattresses, no doubt having the same thoughts that he was. He got up and walked across to a spot where he could look up through the ventilation bricks. He could see a thin ribbon of blue sky, no clouds. As he watched, he saw the vapour trail of a commercial jet leave a white trace across his horribly limited view. He thought of the passengers on the plane, passing overhead, with no idea of what was happening to them a few thousand feet below.

"Morning."

It was Joyce. He was sitting with his back to a dry patch of wall, his legs stretched out and crossed at the ankles.

"Morning."

"Did you sleep?"

"Not really. You?"

"Yes," he said. "I can sleep in most places."

"Even a place like this?"

"I've been in worse."

"You seem pretty calm about everything."

"What's the point in wasting energy when there's nothing you can do? I'd rather save it."

"For what?"

"There'll be a moment when they let their guard down. These boys are not professional. They don't know what they're doing. They don't have a plan and they don't have a routine. There will be a chance. And then I'll get us out."

"So what were you before all this? Military, obviously, but . . ."

"Special forces. SAS."

"And then private security?"

"I did something else in between jobs."

"You're not going to tell me what that was, though."

"That's right."

"Classified?"

"Something like that."

"Your men the same as you?"

"Soldiers. Good ones. The kind of men you'd want in a situation like this. They won't be flustered and they won't panic. They're just like me. They'll wait for a chance. And then they'll take it." He sat up a little straighter. "Your crew, Captain. Are they alright?"

"Do you mean are they handling this? As well as can be expected."

"I mean do I have to worry about any of them giving us up?"

Joe shrugged. "I don't know. I can't speak for them."

"You're the captain, though."

"I don't think that counts for much anymore. We're not at sea."

"No, but you're still their C.O." He leaned in closer and whispered with taut urgency, "And you need to make them listen to you. If the four of us are compromised in any way, your position gets worse, not better. You can't do deals with these people. They don't bargain. It's all about ideology. If we're here, we can get us out. If not, I'd say your odds just got exponentially worse. You understand what I'm saying, Captain?"

"I'm not going to say anything," Joe said. "And these are good men, Joyce. I doubt they will, either."

Joe found he really didn't like Joyce. He had an air of easy arrogance about him that was difficult to stomach. He was happy to let him know that he was a dangerous man, but he wouldn't say why or how. It was all for effect. Joe didn't like his attitude, and he worried that the haughtiness might rub up against their captors the wrong way. He noted to himself that he would have to be ready to ameliorate the friction, because he guessed that it was coming.

They heard the sound of footsteps descending the stone stairs and then the door unlocking. It opened, and Farax and another two men, both of whom were armed, came inside. Farax was holding a large pot which smelt appetising.

"Breakfast," he said, putting the pot down on the floor. "*Behr*. Goat liver. You like this?"

There was also some flat bread, nicely baked and not fried, and some tea. Somali *sheh* was ridiculously sweet, not much more than a sugar solution coloured with brown dye. There were no plates, and so the men tore off pieces of bread and scooped out the liver and onions. It was delicious, and eating it reminded him how hungry he was. They hadn't eaten for over a day. He went back for a second helping.

Farax watched them with a preoccupied expression on his face.

When they were done, he came across to where Joe was sitting and crouched down beside him.

"Now, Joe," he said. "We will talk about what I said on the boat yesterday. There was a man with a long rifle on the boat. He shot my friend. Shot him in head. Killed him. You must tell me who this man is."

Joyce was still next to him. Joe dared not take his eyes from Farax's face for fear of incriminating him.

"We had no long rifles," he said. "I told you already. No rifles."
"You are sure?"

"I am."

"Okay, Joe."

He stood up and nodded to the two men behind him. One of them stood back and levelled his AK. The other stepped forward, grabbed one of the crew by the shoulder and hauled him to his knees. "Up," he ordered, tugging again until the man stood on his feet.

Joe recognised the man. He was middle-aged, one of the chefs in the kitchen. He struggled, the gunman shouting angrily, "I shoot! I shoot!"

"What are you doing?" Joe said.

"Yesterday, an American drone fired a missile at a village in Pakistan. Many dead. Innocent people, dead. The American government must understand that comes at price. Nothing is free, Joe, you understand? Consequences for everything."

The chef was hauled to his feet and dragged to the door. Joe looked into Farax's eyes and saw implacable purpose.

It was the most frightening thing he had ever seen.

"We talk later, Joe, yes? We talk about the man with the long gun."

He left the room, and the door was shut and locked again.

"What are they doing?" Harry Torres said.

"They're moving faster than I thought they would," Joyce said.

"What the fuck does that mean?"

Joyce pressed himself upright and walked across to the other side of the room where the ventilation bricks offered a restricted view into the yard.

Joe followed him. "What *does* that mean?"

"Look," he said.

Joe did. It wasn't easy to make everything out because the view was up high, but as he stood on tiptoe, he could see a large group of fighters, recognisable from the long skirts, or *ma'awiis,* that they were wearing, and then the pasty white legs of the chef as he was dragged between two men to a spot in the middle of the group. He heard Farax's voice, speaking in English, the message difficult to hear at a distance, but the anger and indignation readily apparent.

Farax finished speaking. There was a pause, and then a shrill, blood-curdling cry.

Joyce turned away. "We need to get out of here," he said.

Chapter Eleven

The British government had sent Michael Pope to Marrakech aboard one of the Gulfstream G650s that MI6 leased to get its agents around the world. The sleek jet was parked just off the taxiway, and they were transported to it aboard a courtesy car. The whole process of passing through the airport had been easy. They had proceeded through the terminal building without needing to stop, with just a cursory check of their credentials as they went airside. The rucksack that contained Beatrix's equipment was treated as a diplomatic bag. She had dropped it onto a trolley and pushed it through the terminal without it being scanned or otherwise disturbed. The treatment was familiar to her from her old career.

She had stopped at the duty-free and bought a bottle of water for the flight, and then, seeing a shop that specialised in Islamic dress, she had purchased a niqāb and a jilbāb. *The veil and cloak might prove to be useful,* she thought, as she stuffed them into her bag.

The car drew to a stop, and Beatrix stepped outside into the heat of another fine day. She drew in a deep breath and exhaled, wondering whether she would see the city again, those spectacular mountains, the clamour and bustle of the medina. And then she thought of her daughter, and the reluctance to leave became much more difficult to resist.

She paused at the steps that led up to the open door of the jet.

"All okay?" Pope called down.

"Yes," she said, shrugging her concerns aside. "All fine."

She climbed the steps and entered the jet. There were half a dozen reclining leather seats, two tables and a large flatscreen television fitted to the partition that separated the cockpit from the cabin. Beatrix sat down and strapped herself in, watching pensively as the pilot guided them out onto the runway and fired the twin engines. The jet roared down the runway and launched into the air, cutting to port and climbing steadily. Beatrix watched through the porthole as the Red City dwindled into miniature. She tried to look for the riad, but of course it was impossible. The crazy scramble of streets looked identical from above, and even when she had oriented herself with the broad expanse of Jemma el-Fnaa and the minaret of the Koutoubia mosque, it was still impossible to tell one street from the next.

The pilot banked and the view was replaced by the sandy dunes of the Sahara, occasional oases fringed with lush palms, mud-brick Berber villages and centuries-old kasbahs and, above all of them, the impassive reach of the Atlas Mountains.

"I've got something for you," Pope said.

He fired up the flatscreen with a remote and, using an iPad that was patched through to it, put up a colour photograph of coastal topography. She saw a small town next to a thin white ribbon of sand and then a series of graduating blues as the sea deepened to the east.

"Somalia?" she asked.

He nodded. "This is Barawe. The Americans flew a Global Hawk over it at sixty thousand feet yesterday."

She looked at the screen with renewed interest. Pope flicked through a dozen different pictures. The Hawk was equipped with synthetic aperture radar and electro-optical/infrared sensors. That equipment, combined with the long loiter times that it could stay undetected over an area of interest, could provide superb intelligence.

"It's one hundred and thirty-five miles from Mogadishu. Al-Shabaab took it over after they were forced out of there. The nearest town where government and African Union forces have control is Shalanbood, sixty-eight miles away. To the northeast is the Ambarese training camp for al-Shabaab's foreign fighters. The local military dispatched a unit of officers and support elements to the town in 2012, but they ran into concerted opposition and had to fall back. For all intents and purposes, the terrorists run this town. And that makes it one of the most dangerous places on the planet."

Pope indicated an area close to the beach.

"This house—south of the mosque, here—is where the Americans think the pirates are holding the crew. It's a three-storey beachside property, two hundred metres from the sea on the town's east side. They believe that it is used by *mujahideen* who have gone to Somalia to take up al-Shabaab's cause. They suspect that a Kenyan of Somali origin called Abdulkadir Farax Abdulkadir is in control. He's behind plenty of the activity that's been coming out of Somalia. They think the team responsible for the shopping mall explosion in Kenya came from here. It wouldn't surprise me at all if the SEALs have orders to take him out at the same time they get the hostages out."

"How many fighters?"

"It's a major facility for them," Pope said. "The hostages are a big deal, too, and they'll be on the alert for an attack to get them back. I'd expect plenty."

"Defences?"

"Weight of numbers for the most part. They've got anti-aircraft weapons on the beach, but it's not as if the Americans are going to put Black Hawks over the town after what happened in Mogadishu."

"What chance of the SEALs getting in and out?"

"Hard to say. They'll kick the shit out of the locals, but will it work? I wouldn't want to be a hostage, that's for sure. That's what I meant yesterday—there's a very good chance Joyce doesn't get out of this alive. You might not have to do anything."

She waved it off impatiently. "I need to speak to him. He might know where Control is. And when his time comes, it needs to be me."

"Alright," he said, and then he paused. When he spoke again, it was reluctantly. "I have to be honest with you, Beatrix. If I were planning this operation, I wouldn't do it like this. One agent, on her own, going into a place like that? No backup at all? It's going to be very, very difficult."

"Difficult," Beatrix said. "But not impossible."

Pope grimaced. "There's something else you need to see."

He navigated within the iPad to a video and set it to play.

The footage showed a wide yard with a building made from white coral behind it. The flag of al-Shabaab had been hung on the wall, and a group of men were gathered in front of the camera in a loose semi-circle. They were all armed with AK-47s, and their faces were obscured by red-and-white-chequered *kufiyas*, the Arab scarves that distinguished the terrorist faction.

"That's the house in Barawe?"

"Just watch."

The footage was being filmed on a digital camera, but it was shoulder mounted and a little unstable. Beatrix watched as the semi-circle parted and three men came to the front. Two were dragging a third, his feet trailing behind him. It looked as if he had been beaten.

"Who is he?"

"One of the crew. A chef."

"When is this?"

"Yesterday. They had it up on YouTube until it was pulled."

One of the men in the crowd came forward, stepping between the beaten man and the camera. The *kufiya* obscured his face save for his eyes.

He spoke into the camera: "My name is Abdulkadir Farax Abdulkadir and I am a representative of al-Shabaab in Somalia. We will strike Americans where it hurts the most, turn their cities into graveyards, and rivers of blood will flow wherever they seek to make their incursions into Muslim lands. The American government's decision to keep their invading forces in Afghanistan and Iraq is an indication that they haven't yet learnt their lessons from the other attacks that we have mounted against them. The American government is now inviting unprecedented levels of insecurity, bloodshed and destruction. This is a demonstration of the punishment that we shall mete out to any representative of the unbelieving crusaders we capture."

Abdulkadir stepped aside as the prisoner was dragged forward. One of the other men gave him a machete and he moved behind the beaten man, knotted his fist in his hair and yanked his head back to expose his throat.

"We will execute one hostage every day until the last Zionist boot has left holy Islamic soil, Insha'Allah."

He brought the machete across the man's throat.

Pope paused the footage before it could continue.

"You know the kind of men they are. They'll do it. The Americans are going to try once to get the hostages away. If the SEALs don't think it can be done without taking heavy casualties, they'll pull back."

"And then?"

"And then there is Plan B. The Americans have an expeditionary base in Djibouti. USAFRICOM. They've got Reapers and Predators up there. If the SEALs have to pull out, they'll light the house up, call in an air strike and drop a five-hundred-pound JDAM onto it. Boom. They'll wipe it off the map."

"And kill the hostages?"

"From what I hear, the President has already signed it off. If it gets to that, then they're all dead anyway. It'd be a mercy killing."

Beatrix chewed on that. It was difficult enough as it was and now she had a deadline to contend with, too.

"Are the SEALs in theatre?"

"Inbound right now on a C-5 Galaxy. They've got a Mark V insertion boat with them and they're going to jump in range of the USS *Tortuga*. That'll get them closer. They'll ride the Mark V most of the rest of the way and then they'll come ashore on RIBs. You know how that works. Very stealthy."

"When?"

"The next couple of days is what I'm hearing."

"Alright," she said.

"What are you going to do?"

"I can't think of a better distraction than a gun battle. I'm going to take advantage of it."

Chapter Twelve

Beatrix watched through the window of the Gulfstream as they descended towards the airport at Dadaab. They were far to the east of Nairobi in the high desert, the single asphalt runway glittering like a ribbon of mercury as the pilot circled to line up with it. The pilot announced that they were on approach and Beatrix buckled up. The airport became clearer as they descended. Only Kenya Airways flew out of the facility, flying domestic hops around the country. There were a couple of turbo-props parked next to the ramshackle terminal building.

As they descended she saw the enormous refugee camp that had gathered on the edge of the city. It had been built twenty years before, originally to accommodate the human detritus that had been pushed out of Somalia by the civil war, but in the time since then, nothing had been done to solve the problem. It had lingered, metastasising until it was a seething mass of three hundred thousand souls. It was the largest camp in the world and still it was growing. It was a vivid reminder that Somalia was a failed state, that its problems kept its own citizens away and that, above all else, it was a dangerous place.

And Beatrix intended to drive right into the black heart of it.

She looked across the cabin at Pope. He was gazing out the window, too, a slightly pensive expression on his face. He would try to persuade her again to choose a different course, she was sure of that.

And she would deny him.

She felt the buzz of an old excitement tickling the hairs on the back of her neck. It was a familiar sensation, the anticipation of imminent action, but this time the edge was whetted by the knowledge that this particular target was personal, very deserving, and long overdue.

Three soldiers from the Kenya Defence Forces were waiting for them as they disembarked. Pope introduced himself to the corporal. Beatrix left her Oakleys on and Pope did not introduce her. It was much better that way. The corporal led them to the old Toyota Land Cruiser that was parked on the edge of the strip. It was at least twenty years old and was in a bit of a state: the tyres were bald in several places, the bodywork was festooned with rust and the front lamp housings were both broken. When Beatrix opened the hood, she saw that the radiator and engine were corroded and smothered in grease. The blackened firewall indicated that there had been a problem with overheating.

"As requested," the corporal said. "Fully serviced and fuelled. And you have another twenty gallons in the back."

She followed him around to look: four five-gallon jerry cans had been roped into the wide cargo area.

"Thank you," Pope replied.

Beatrix's disappointment must have been palpable. The soldier turned to her and said, "It is suitable?"

"Yes," she said, finding a little enthusiasm. "I'm sure it will be perfect."

Pope thanked the corporal again.

Beatrix waited until he was out of earshot before speaking. "He thinks this rust bucket is going to get me four hundred miles?"

"Best I could do on short notice," he replied.

"They gave it to us?"

"No. Her Majesty bought it for you."

"I don't know." She rapped a knuckle on the hood. "As long as it runs, I suppose it'll do."

"Are you sure you want to do this?"

"Yes," she said.

"I could speak to the Americans—"

"No," she said. "Thanks, but I'll take my chances."

They went around to the front of the Land Cruiser, Pope slapping the bonnet with the palm of his hand. "Alright then. Good luck."

Beatrix pulled herself into the jeep and shut the door. "Thanks for your help. I appreciate it."

"Be lucky."

Beatrix turned the ignition and gunned the engine. It rumbled to life, shaking the hood, and sounded healthy enough. It was just over four hundred miles from Dadaab to Barawe. The tank held fifteen gallons, and she estimated that the jeep would do twenty miles to the gallon. The tank would run dry after she was just over three quarters of the way there, but she could refill it from the jerry cans, and that should be enough to get her to her destination. There ought to be enough left to put at least a little distance between herself and the town after she accomplished her mission. She would have to find more fuel on the way back, but she would worry about that when the time came.

She crunched the gearbox into first and rolled away. Pope shielded his eyes against the sharp morning rays as she went by and then raised his hand in farewell. She gave a curt nod in response.

She rolled out of the airport and south towards the A3. It ran west to east from Nairobi to the border. She edged the jeep up to fifty miles an hour. She guessed the roads would be decent enough until she got to the crossing, but after that, it would be a lottery. If she could maintain an average speed of fifty she would be at the coast in eight hours.

It was a hot day, and the air that blew over the windscreen and over her was warm. She looked at her watch: it was a little past eight in the morning. She would be in Barawe by the early evening.

Chapter Thirteen

P ope watched Beatrix drive away. He wondered for the hundredth time whether he was doing the right thing. This was what Beatrix wanted, he reminded himself. All he had done was to present her with the intelligence. She had insisted on how things would play out from here.

There were wheels within wheels, just like there always were, but she was being put into a position to do what she wanted to do.

But it was still difficult to accept that his orders were pure.

The sun battered down as he turned and went back to the jet. He collected his suitcase and returned to the airstrip, finding his way back to the corporal from the KDF.

"Do you know where they are?" he asked the man.

The clatter of noise that became audible in the distance and then steadily grew louder was his answer.

He turned towards the east and watched as the helicopter appeared through the haze, flying low and fast. The corporal led him out onto the airstrip as the chopper breached the airport perimeter, flared up as it killed its speed and then descended, the rotor wash generating a cloud of sand and grit.

It was an MH-60S Knighthawk, the multi-mission platform that the US Navy deployed for combat search and rescue, vertical replenishment, special warfare support and mine countermeasures. The turbines whined, not winding down. They weren't stopping long.

Pope thanked the corporal again and jogged across the airstrip, pressing his shades against his face as the miniature sandstorm whipped around him. The side door of the Knighthawk slid back, and Pope reached up to take the hand of the Navy flyer inside.

"Good morning, sir," the man said.

"Morning."

"We're just going to fill up, and then we'll be on our way."

The Knighthawk was designed around the Black Hawk's airframe, and Pope was familiar with the robust and versatile aircraft from his operational days. The pilot and co-pilot sat side by side on armour-protected seats. The crew member who had helped Pope inside took his seat next to the forward cabin window. Pope sat down in one of the cabin's bucket seats and strapped himself in. He watched through the glass cockpit as an airport tanker truck pulled alongside and the third crewman worked with the ground crew to refill the Knighthawk's tanks.

"We all set?" the co-pilot called back as he clambered back inside.

Pope nodded. "Let's go."

The twin T700-GE-401C turboshaft engines powered up again, filling the cabin with noise. Pope took the headphones that were hanging from a hook on the side of the seat and slipped them over his ears. He watched through the gunner's window as the chopper rose up, the terminal building sliding out of sight.

The nose dipped as the helicopter picked up speed, heading east. Pope looked down at the fast-moving terrain below, at the road that led from Dadaab to Somalia, and wondered whether he might see the Land Cruiser with Beatrix inside, rushing headlong into the most dangerous failed state on earth.

⌣

They flew east and then southeast, staying on the Kenyan side of the border until they reached the sea. The pilot turned to the north, and they flew on, the coast of Somalia just visible on the port side of the aircraft. It was six hundred miles from Dadaab to their destination, but a Knighthawk with a full tank of fuel had plenty of range.

The pilot's voice came over the headphones: "We're coming in now. On deck in five minutes."

Pope saw the big warship five hundred metres ahead of them. She was the USS *Tortuga*, a Whidbey Island–class landing ship that belonged to the US Navy's Amphibious Group. As they drew closer, Pope could see the distinctive welldeck to stern, the door raised and the interior not yet flooded.

The Knighthawk slowed and descended carefully, the pilot positioning it precisely to land on the small flight deck. The wheels touched down with a gentle bump as the pilot powered down the engines and started to work through the post-flight checks.

Pope unstrapped himself as the door was opened from the outside by a stocky sailor wearing a utility uniform with a blue and grey digital print pattern.

"Request permission to come aboard," Pope said.

The man reached up his hand to help him down. "Good to meet you, Captain Pope."

He took the man's hand and jumped down to the deck. The briny tang of the sea filled his nostrils, and the damp breeze was refreshing. He turned to the west and gazed out. They were twenty miles from land, too far out to be seen from here.

"I'm Lieutenant Commander Shawn McMahon, officer in charge of the on-board operation."

"Good to meet you," he said, raising his voice to be heard above the whine of the fading engines.

"Likewise. If you'll follow me, Captain."

They walked away from the Knighthawk towards the middle of the ship.

"Good trip?"

"Nice and easy. Any updates?"

McMahon shook his head. "Nothing much. There's a Global Hawk on station at sixty thousand feet, and they've re-tasked a couple of NSA satellites so we've got eyes on the town. They've holed up in the house on the coast. You've seen the pictures?"

"Yes. The hostages?"

"They haven't killed any more of them, if that's what you mean."

"Just a matter of time."

"I think so, too."

"When did you get here?"

"Six hours ago. We jumped in, got picked up and my men are getting themselves ready now."

McMahon opened a door, and they went inside the ship.

"Do you need anything now, sir?"

"Can you show me to my room? I need to make a call."

"Sure."

Pope had been assigned officers' quarters. It was a small room, with everything packed in tight: six curtained bunks with rows of drawers beneath them, small stainless steel sinks and, through a bulkhead, a rec room with a TV, some chairs, a pull-out metal desk and lockers. The turgid, stale air was circulated by a fan.

He put his suitcase on the bed, unlatched it, opened it and took out the equipment that he needed. He left the satphone on the bed and switched on the multi-channel bug detector. Pope was ostensibly a friend aboard the *Tortuga,* but he was not naïve enough to think that the privacy of his communications would be respected. There was too much at stake for niceties like that.

The detector had been designed in the labs in the basement of the MI6 building next to the Thames and was good to detect bugs transmitting on practically any frequency. He directed it around the small room until the unit buzzed gently, the numbers on the readout stopping at ninety, indicating a WiFi listening device. He used the scanner to isolate the signal, eventually finding the little transmitter inside the plug that powered the TV in the rec room. He carefully disassembled the housing and withdrew the bug.

He went back into the other room, took the satphone from its case and switched it on. It used military encryption, and he was as confident as he could be that, if he was still being eavesdropped on, his call would be secure.

He sat on the edge of the nearest bed and dialled the number he wanted.

"Global Logistics," the woman at the end of the line intoned. "How may I direct your call?"

"This is Michael Pope," he said. "I'd like to speak to the managing director, please."

It was standard procedure. Global Logistics was the cover for Group Fifteen.

"Just connecting you now, Mr Pope."

The line was poor quality, but despite that, the next voice was distinctive and easily recognised. "Hello, Pope. Can you hear me?"

The voice belonged to Sir Benjamin Stone, the man otherwise known as "C."

"Yes, sir. Loud and clear."

"Where are you?"

He spoke quietly. "Aboard the ship."

"Very good. How did it go?"

"All to plan."

"She got where she needed to go?"

"I took her to Kenya, as we discussed. Whether she can get across the border or not is something for her. We've done all we can to help."

C was quiet for a moment. "She's in play now. The random element. Should make things interesting."

"Quite so."

Pope had found out as much about Stone as he could. He was his superior, after all, and Pope liked to know who he was working with. Control going rogue had thrown the intelligence community into confusion, and Stone's predecessor had been forced to fall on his sword. It was Stone who had visited him in hospital while he was convalescing to offer him the job as the head of Group Fifteen.

Little was known about Stone, at least publicly. He had been born in Warwick, studied physics and philosophy and then spent time at Harvard. He joined the Foreign and Commonwealth Office and made fast progress through the ranks, serving as a political officer in Damascus and then as a desk officer in the European Union Department. He worked in Washington for a time, and then became foreign affairs advisor to the prime minister. He was ambassador to Egypt and a special representative in Baghdad. The off-the-record information that Pope had uncovered revealed surprisingly little more than what was already known. Stone liked tennis. He liked to cook. He liked horses.

Only one thing was constant from all the information that he uncovered: Benjamin Stone was a careerist, he was brilliant, he had incredible connections—and he was utterly untrustworthy.

"How was she?" Stone asked him now.

"Determined, sir."

"Her state of mind?"

"Very focussed."

"She better be."

"Do the Americans know about her?"

"Not specifically. They know we have an asset in play. That's it."

Pope frowned. "Shouldn't we front up now, sir?"

"Let them start the operation first."

"Really? It might be better for her if they knew everything."

"Yes," Stone said, his irritation obvious, "it probably would, but it's not better for us, is it? What if they disagree? They could pull the whole bloody thing if they think we're interfering. It'll just cause a headache. We've decided this is the way we're going to do it, and we're not changing tack now. They'll know when they need to know and not before."

"Yes, sir."

"It's very useful that she came to you, Pope. We can't leave Control in play like this. We need to find him. He's much too dangerous. The secrets he has, God only knows what the Chinese would do if they knew he was out there. The Russians. The bloody *Americans*. You think she'll be able to get to him?"

"She wants him more than you do, sir. If anyone can do it, she can."

"And, of course, she can use methods that oversight committees might get a little, well, squeamish about."

Stone was the kind of operator that Pope had no time for. He had ridden a desk all of his career, never once dirtying his hands with the reality of modern intelligence, and yet he was blithely happy to send agents into the field with scant regard for their safety. Not telling the SEALs about Beatrix was a case in point. That kind of leadership might have worked with Pope's predecessor, but he had promised himself that it would not work with him. He would do everything he could to watch over her.

"I'll keep you posted, sir."

"Very good, Pope. Please do."

"Yes, sir," he said, but C. had already ended the call, and the handset was full of static.

Chapter Fourteen

I t took Beatrix two hours to reach the border. The road from Dadaab was like a broad, parched river bed. The surface had been so abused over the years that now it felt as if she was driving in a shallow bowl flanked by riverbanks and layered in different textures of sand, from the rock-hard to the soft desert grains.

She passed through a handful of scattered villages, wattle huts where local tribes made their homes. The road crested a final hill and then descended to a checkpoint with a pair of mesh gates closed across it. A dilapidated fence stretched away for a hundred feet in both directions, and a wooden door had been hung between posts just next to a ramshackle gatehouse. A mobile phone mast stood ten yards behind the gatehouse, and half a dozen armed soldiers faced each other on either side. Beatrix stopped the jeep while she was still three hundred yards away and assessed her next move.

The Kenyans looked tough and fierce, but their attention was focussed to the north. It must have been different here, once, before the resurgence of the jihadist fighters in the mangrove swamps just across the border. There had been many instances of hostile incursions, culminating in the attack on the shopping mall in Nairobi that had killed so many people not long before. This was one of the most dangerous border crossings in the world, and the young soldiers would have been hopelessly inadequate if al-Shabaab came at them in numbers. That must have been the reason behind the obvious surliness with which they examined those coming south.

On the other side of the gate, the Somali guards were more relaxed, yet she couldn't ignore their AK-47s. They laughed and joked and had an easy, natural arrogance that Beatrix thought might well be dangerous. She had been hoping for a quieter crossing, but that was not going to be possible here. Attitudes towards women were prehistoric among the jihadists, and she was sure that there would be an incident if she tried to make her way across the line here.

Beatrix had made a career out of listening to her gut, and she wasn't about to stop now.

She turned around and drove the sixty kilometres back to Dadaab.

⁓

The roads quickly became busy with people and traffic, and she had to lean on the horn several times to clear stray donkeys from her path. She drove into the enormous refugee camp. There were structures made of wood, canvas and sheeting material with the letters "USA" printed on them. The streets disappeared off in all directions, some servicing neat lines of UN tents and others picking paths through accommodations laid out haphazardly, with no sense or design. It was nothing like the other refugee camps Beatrix had seen. This one had an air of dogged permanence about it, and the facilities that would be associated with a town of a similar size had all sprung up like mushrooms on a compost heap: shops, bars, makeshift offices.

Beatrix found her way to the UNHCR Reception Centre in Dagahaley and asked for directions to somewhere she could stay for the night. The clerk behind the desk gave her directions to a small area where tents could be hired for a few pennies. She drove the short distance to the facility and took one.

She hoisted her rucksack over her shoulder and went out again into the dusty street. The camp was labyrinthine. An open sewer trickled alongside the gutter, choked here and there with dung and fetid strips of plastic. There was a camel butcher who advertised that, for religious reasons, he only slaughtered his animals at 3:00 a.m. Next to that was the Candaalo Beauty Salon, where you could have your hair braided and cut and henna tattoos applied. She passed men and women who were bedding down in the doorways of their tents, the better to watch the stars above and the people who passed by.

She stopped a local for directions and walked on for a hundred yards until she found the metal shack that he had described. It was called the Sabrina Hotel and was in the Ifo 2 area of the camp. A metal sign daubed with black paint greeted visitors in English and Arabic "with open hands."

She pushed her way through the door into just the kind of bar she was looking for. Most of it was open, with a collection of mismatched patio chairs and tables spread out across a dusty yard. The bar itself was fashioned within the corrugated tin walls, a long plank of wood suspended on two piles of bricks with a collection of bottles arranged on another shelf behind it. Beatrix approached and ordered a beer. The bartender handed her a lukewarm bottle of Tusker Premium, and she paid for it with five dollars.

"Anything else?" he asked her when he noticed that she was looking at him.

"You might be able to help me," she said. "I'm looking for a guide."

"A guide for what?"

"I need to get into Somalia."

"I doubt it."

"Unofficially."

"Why would you want to do something like that?"

"I'm a journalist," she explained. "I'm writing a story about the jihadists."

"Then you're crazy."

She smiled patiently at him. "I need to be over there to write what I need to write, and I won't be able to explain myself if I have to cross at a checkpoint. They won't let me in."

"For which you should be grateful. You know what it is like over there, yes? No place for a lady."

"Can you help me?"

"I can't," he said, and turned away.

She stayed at the bar and sipped the beer. The bartender looked over at her now and again, and she made sure to hold his gaze.

After ten minutes she finished her beer, and when he was looking in her direction, she tapped her finger on it.

"Yes?" he said.

"Another."

He nodded and popped the top of a second bottle. She paid him again.

"I know you can help me," she said.

"I don't know what you're talking about."

"There's a hundred dollars in it for you."

She slid a note across the bar.

He paused.

"Come on. It's my funeral, right?"

"You want a smuggler."

She kept her hand across the note. "I suppose I do. You know any?"

"In a place like this? Of course. I know many."

"So you can help."

"Yes."

She had expected to have to grease a palm or two, and it was going to be necessary here. He might be spinning her a line, but what choice did she have? She was a fish out of water. She lifted her hand.

He folded and pocketed the bill. "Wait at the bar. The man I am thinking of usually arrives at ten."

"Fine," she said.

She drank the second beer, grateful for the moisture in her dry throat, and was about to start a third when she noticed the bartender speaking to a newcomer at the other side of the bar. They looked over at her, and she held their eyes.

The newcomer came across and stood before her.

"My name is Bashir," he said.

"Beatrix."

She looked at him: average height, a mouthful of yellowing teeth, hair that was as black as pitch. He was dressed in Levis and a pair of cowboy boots, ostentatiously expensive in a bar where everyone else was dressed in dirty T-shirts, shorts and flip-flops.

"My friend tells me you want to get into Somalia."

"Yes."

"And you are a journalist?"

"That's right," she said impatiently. "Can you help me?"

"It is a dangerous thing you ask."

"That's why I'll pay you a thousand dollars. Can you do it?"

"I can. You are lucky, madam. I am from the Boni tribe. My forefathers were hunter-gatherers on the border. They knew the land very well. They would whistle to the birds who would guide them to wild honey in the acacia trees."

She flicked a hand at his prosperous dress. "I'm guessing you're not much into the honey business."

He laughed. "Indeed not. I am a trader. I take mangos from Somalia and sell them in Kenya, and then I take bottled water from Kenya and sell it in Somalia. I do this again and again. Taxes and bribes are common at the border, and I try to keep my expenses to a minimum. So, yes, I am very familiar with crossing. Where do you mean to go?"

"Barawe."

He whistled through his teeth. "That will not be cheap. Barawe is a very dangerous place. The jihadists control it. A thousand dollars will not be enough."

"How much?"

"Five thousand. All before."

"Half before, half on arrival."

He spread his hands. "Then I cannot help you."

Beatrix called his bluff. "Fair enough." She stood.

He let her take three steps away from the bar before he called her back.

"Very well. Three thousand now, two thousand on arrival. I am taking a very big risk, madam."

"Fine. How do we do it?"

"I have a truck. I am taking a load of water tomorrow. Early morning. Can you travel then?"

"Just tell me where to be."

Beatrix walked back to the campsite. The night was hot, still and stifling, and there was an edge of incipient violence in the dark corners and rowdy bars. She stopped at a roadside shack for a meal of beans and rice and watched the Somali market alongside, which was still open. It reminded her of a scene out of Aladdin. Children rode mule carts and hit the mules with long reeds to make them go faster. Goats chased each other. Women lay face down on prayer mats. A small crowd of kids collected around her and stood watching her eating as if it was something that they had never seen before. They stared unabashedly and did not avert their eyes when she looked at them. "Salaam," she said. One of the children spoke pidgin English and introduced himself. She asked all of them their names, and then the conversation fell silent. They scattered and left her to finish her meal alone.

She set off again. A large UN truck with a canvas-covered back rumbled by, and the same group of children appeared out of nowhere to chase after it. She was a little surprised that the Land Cruiser was where she had left it. She went into her tent, took out a bottle of water and her morphine and drank down another two pills. The ache was steady now, almost constant, and she knew that the exertion of the next few days would exacerbate it further.

Nothing much that she could do about that.

She arranged her mosquito net and tried to ignore the roaches that scuttled beneath the sides of the tent, looking for food.

Sleep, when it came, was not particularly refreshing.

Chapter Fifteen

Beatrix was already awake when the early morning call to prayer began to sound over the malfunctioning loudspeakers at the mosque that served this part of the camp. She rose and found her way to the outdoor shower, where she stayed under the cold water for longer than usual because she didn't know when she would be able to do it again. The tattoo on her shoulder had healed nicely, the colours particularly vivid now that the inflammation had receded. She dressed in a pair of white trousers and a sleeveless T-shirt, hauled her rucksack onto her shoulder and quietly left the tents.

Veins of light were just beginning to streak the royal-blue sky and the air, for now at least, was cold.

Bashir said that he knew a place where she could park the Land Cruiser safely. It was a recessed space between two tents, and, he said, a dollar a day would see the locals keep an eye on it. Beatrix had no reason to doubt their probity, and she was further reassured when she was hailed by an elderly woman who was sitting in the dust before the open awning of her tent. In truth, having the vehicle here and in one piece was useful, but not essential. She did not know whether she would exfiltrate through Kenya or whether she might, for example, head north to Ethiopia. She had determined to solve that particular problem as it played out.

She was locking the Land Cruiser as a large, beaten-up truck wheezed up and parked alongside her.

Bashir opened the door and jumped down.

"Good morning," he said.

"Morning."

"Are you ready?"

"Yes."

"Money, please."

She gave him two bundles of notes, and he made a show of thumbing through them and counting.

"Alright," he said. "Three thousand. It is here. Two thousand later. But you are still sure? You want to do this?"

"Can we just get going? I want to get over there as quickly as we can."

They drove off. The camp was quieter, resting, although far from still. Bashir drove carefully until they were out on the main road and headed east, following the Garissa Road just as she had followed it yesterday, and then he accelerated. Beatrix looked out of the window and saw the red corona of the sun slowly rising above the prairie. Two tall giraffes kicked up the dust as they galloped with elegant nonchalance through the rough, drought-resistant vegetation on the left-hand side of the road. Five minutes later, he had to stop to allow a herd of camels to wander aimlessly across their way.

"This story," he said as he settled back in the seat. "What is it about?"

"How women are treated in Somalia."

"I can tell you that. Not well. Do you still need to go?"

"What do you know about al-Shabaab ?"

"Just that they are very bad. Very violent men. You would be wise to avoid them."

"But Barawe is their stronghold?"

"They had more, once. You know the civil war in Somalia?" She said that she did. "A most brutal war. The Shabaab flourished, like weeds. They had most of the south until the Kenyans and the Ethiopians and the USA decided they were not good. They still make it impossible for aid to get into the country. You saw Dadaab. It is not a pleasant place to live. Al-Shabaab have murdered aid workers, and those they do not kill, they tax. It is better now, and they have been pushed back, but Barawe is not a safe place."

"For you or for me?"

"For us both. I will drive you to outside the town. If you want to go farther, you must walk. It is too dangerous to take the truck farther than that."

Chapter Sixteen

They had talked about trying to resist after seeing what had happened to the chef. Joe had sent the steward to the door to make sure that they were not overheard and then he had started the discussion.

"What are we going to do?"

"I know what we can't do," Barry Miller said. "I'm damn sure we can't do nothing. They'll just work their way through us until there ain't no one left."

"Alright," Harry Torres said. "We try and overpower them. When they come in with our food. They only come down in fours now. We position a couple of us near the door, and when they come in, we rush them. There's more of us than there are of them."

"Yeah," Nelson said. "And they've got Kalashnikovs."

"So a couple of us are going to have to suck it up for the team. If it's a question of going out like that or going out like *that*", he pointed up towards the courtyard, "then I know which way I'd prefer."

"What then?"

"We take the guns and shoot our way out. Maybe it doesn't work. Maybe we all get shot. But if it's a choice, do nothing or fight, then I'm fighting."

There was a low mumble of assent.

"Alright," Joe said. "Anyone got a better idea?"

"What about them?" Torres asked, indicating the Manage Risk operatives. They had taken no part in the discussion. Rather, they kept to themselves, talking quietly.

"Yeah, Joe," Miller said angrily. "What *about* them? They're the fricking soldiers and they ain't doing jack."

"I've got to say, Joe," Torres added, "seems to me that one thing we haven't talked about is giving them what they want."

"What do you mean?"

"I mean we're all going to die if we just sit here and keep quiet, right? We know what they want. It's a shame and all, but those boys aren't crew and they're not friends. I think we've got to consider whether we should tell Farax that those guys are the soldiers they want. I mean, come on, it's not like he doesn't already know. You've seen the way he looked at them. They look like soldiers—it's obvious. He just wants you to tell him."

"I'm not doing that," Joe said firmly. "We're all in the same mess here. I don't see that we're in a position where we can just hand someone over, knowing that he'll get taken up there and killed. That's not moral, Harry. You could even say that'd be murder."

"Bull*shit*," Miller said. "Murder? What you been smoking, Captain? Come on, look at 'em. They're not even interested in taking part in this discussion. And you think they wouldn't hand us over to the Somalis if the roles were reversed?"

"You don't know that. And it doesn't matter what they would or wouldn't do. There's a right way and a wrong way to do things, and pointing the finger at them is the wrong way. One hundred per cent wrong. It'd bring us down to the same level as Farax. I'm not doing it."

"I'm sorry, Skip, you're wrong."

The other men grumbled their agreement. Joe knew that his authority was tenuous. They weren't aboard ship: they were all in the same hole together. It was only his residual command that was keeping them all in line. If he flouted their wishes, that wouldn't be relevant for very long.

"Look, I'll talk to them, alright? Chances are they know what they're doing and they've got something in hand they just haven't told us about yet. But I'll see what they say."

The Somalis appeared with their food ten minutes later. Joe looked at Harry Torres and Barry Miller and gave a quick, stern shake of his head. Not yet. They both nodded. It was goat stew again and they ate it quietly, determinedly, and Joe knew that he was on a countdown. The next time they wouldn't agree with him so easily.

He approached Joyce after they had eaten.

"Alright?"

"Captain."

"The men have been talking."

"We noticed."

"They want to do something. They don't want to just wait."

"What do you want?"

"Truthfully? I can see where they're coming from."

He leaned forward. "So what's the plan?"

"We wait for them to come back down again and jump them."

Joyce shook his head and laughed bitterly, as if that were something that a child had come up with.

"What?" Joe said, his cheeks reddening with indignation.

"Look where we are," he said. "We're in a basement. The only way out is through that door and then up the stairs."

"But we'd have a gun. Two, probably."

"You know how many rounds you get in an AK?"

"No."

"Thirty. You could chew through that in ten seconds. You know how easy it would be for them to take us down? All they'd need to do is wait." He shook his head, correcting himself. "No. They wouldn't even need to wait. Did you notice what some of them had on their belts?"

Joe shook his head.

"Grenades. They've got grenades. They could very easily just roll a couple of them down into here and blow the shit out of all of us. Confined space like this, you wouldn't believe what the shrapnel from a grenade can do."

"You said you were going to do something."

"Yes, and we've talked about it. We're thinking of a way."

"When? We don't have the luxury of time, do we?"

"We're thinking of a way," he repeated. "You have to be patient."

"There's no time for that." Joe shook his head vehemently. "Look, you don't have to take part if you don't want to. Just stay out of the way and leave it to us."

"I can't let you do something stupid like that. You'll get us all killed."

There it was, that arrogance again. "You can't *let* me? What does that mean?"

"It means that if you try and do something idiotic, we'll stop you."

Joe kept his voice low. He didn't want to argue in front of the others. "Who made you in charge?"

"You think it should be you?"

"No, but . . ."

"You're out of your depth here."

"So what's your big idea? We'll put it to a vote."

"Don't be an idiot."

"We'll see what the others say, shall we?"

Joe started to get up, but Joyce reached across to him and rested his fingers lightly on his arm, in the fleshy part just above the elbow. He squeezed, just a little, and just with a couple of fingers, but the jolt of pain that shrieked up Joe's arm was dizzying. He sat down again, leaning back heavily. Joyce released his grip. No one else had noticed what had just happened.

"Just relax, Captain. Take it easy. You need to trust me. I told you before, I know what I'm doing. I'm not going to wait here for them to slaughter us all. And I'm not going to let you do something that will get us all killed. I *will* get us out."

━━━━━⌣━━━━━

They came down as the sun rose, the light filtering down through the ventilation bricks slowly gaining strength. Farax was in the front, again, but there were four others with him. Two of the men had AKs, as they had before, and another two had pistols. The Somalis knew that they would have to be more careful this time because there would be no surprises about what they had come down to do. The men with the rifles stayed at the door, training their weapons on the hostages, and Farax came forward, knelt before Joe.

When he spoke, his voice was so soft and gentle that Joe could almost forget the hateful diatribe that he had heard from the yard outside before the chef was murdered.

"I ask again. Who had the long gun, Captain?"

"I told you. There were no snipers."

"But that is not true. We know that your employer had a contract with a company to provide security to your ship. The company is called Manage Risk. You have heard of them?"

"No, I have not."

"I think that you have. We know that this company has provided security for other ships operating in the Arabian Sea. Your
employer has used them many times before, for example. I know
them, too. I will tell you about an incident, one in particular that
I remember very well. I was aboard a boat with my brothers. We
were seeking to take a ship much like yours. We attached our
ladders, but then as we tried to climb aboard, soldiers appeared and
shot my brothers in cold blood. I was at the bottom of the ladder.
I dived into the water as my brothers fell from the ladder. The
soldiers fired at the bodies for a minute. They all died, Captain.
I pretended to be dead, floating with the bodies, in their blood,
until the ship was on the horizon and I could be collected. The
sharks had the others."

"I'm sorry, Farax, but you can't expect me to be sympathetic."

His jaw clenched and there was a momentary flash in his eye
that reminded Joe of his oratory. "No, Captain, I do not expect your
sympathy. But when it is being reported on Western television that
the ship included operatives from Manage Risk, perhaps now you
will understand why it is a gift from Allah that your crew should
contain men from this company." He stood and pointed to where
Joyce and the three men under his command sat. "It is easy to tell a
soldier from a sailor, Captain. I know these are the men. I wish to
make an example of the one who fired the long gun. You will tell me
who it was, or we will take one member of your crew until you do.
I leave it to you. A matter for your conscience."

Joe tried to stand, but one of the guards swung his rifle around,
shaking his head. "You want me to give a man up to die?"

"It is justice. Who was it, Captain? This is your last chance
today. Someone must die. Who is it to be?"

Joe felt hot vomit rising in his gorge. "I . . . I can't tell you what
I don't know."

"Very well." Farax rose quickly. "Him," he said, pointing roughly at Ryan Nelson.

The two men with pistols hurried forward, took Nelson by the elbows and dragged him away from the wall. He struggled and screamed, his sneakers scrabbling against the rough basement floor, but they were too strong for him. They looped their arms beneath his shoulders and heaved him to the door and then away up the stairs.

"No," Joe yelled out, lunging towards the door.

"No, Captain," Farax said. The men with the AKs aimed them at him. He stopped. He had no doubt that they would shoot.

"Don't do this, Farax."

"What choice have you given me? I will see you later, Captain. I will pray that Allah gives you the gift of wisdom."

Farax left the room. The door closed behind him.

Chapter Seventeen

They made excellent progress. It was early and the roads were empty, the sixty kilometres to the border gradually disappearing beneath the wheels of the truck.

They approached a small settlement, and Bashir took his foot off the gas and glided in to the side of the road.

"What are we doing?"

"We will stop here. This is a Boni village. My tribe. You will have a cup of tea and some breakfast?"

Beatrix followed Bashir along a narrow path between coconut trees. The soft sand gave under the soles of her boots, pitching her about. The village was tiny. The Boni encampment comprised a few wattle huts and other shelters made of branches and plastic. It was pathetic, even compared to the squalor of the camp. Bashir explained, superfluously, that life was difficult for them here. The brackish well was far away, decent firewood was scarce and the children often went hungry.

One of the tents seemed to offer food and drink, and Bashir collected two cups of scalding hot masala tea. Beatrix's feet were aching, and the morphine wasn't helping. She took off her boots and massaged the soles. When she rested them, the sand burned her skin. It was only early, but the sun was already as hot as a poker, advancing upwards with relentless purpose. A woman came out of the hut with two slices of white bread, and Beatrix ate hers as a male colobus monkey with bright blue balls watched, the monkey making a grab for the crumbs that scattered at her feet.

They set off again. Beatrix recognised the road from before, but a couple of kilometres from the checkpoint, Bashir swung the wheel and turned off the road. He followed a narrow track, just wide enough for the truck to pass, and skirted to the east and then back to the north.

"What is this?" Beatrix asked.

"It is a *panya*. A smuggler's run."

The track cut deeper and deeper into the brush. The surface was much worse than the Garissa Road, just a rough track that swung left and right between the low bushes. Sometimes the rocks would change into a smoother, sandier surface, and Bashir could accelerate a little. That was unusual, though, and progress was generally slow. The stony outcrops demanded care and attention, and the occasional diversion; they followed paths that were barely even tracks until the obstacles were cleared. The branches scraped against the side of the truck and the windows, and the suspension clanked and groaned as they bumped into and out of ditches and depressions. Bashir was cheerful throughout it all, singing along to Somali music on the radio.

After thirty minutes they heard another engine, and Beatrix held her breath until she saw it was another truck. This one was designed for cattle, but it was carrying people in the back. Bashir pulled into a passing point and let the truck go by. Beatrix saw a dozen pairs of eyes staring at them as the truck bounced along the road, and pairs of hands gripping the wooden slats.

"They go to Dabaab," Bashir said. "One thousand a day arrive in the camp. Al-Shabaab are emptying the country."

Bashir fetched them both bottles of water from the back of the truck, and they drank until the noise of the engine had receded and the birdsong had started up again.

They climbed more sharply, the truck's engine wheezing from the effort, eventually turning into a dried-out wadi and following its route up to a ridge. The sides of the wadi were taller than the truck, and for a moment, it felt as if they were inside a tunnel. Then, after a short ascent, the wadi disappeared, and a plateau levelled out around them.

Bashir stopped the truck.

Beatrix looked out from their elevated position. She could see wide stretches of sand, areas of low scrub and denser vegetation that must have been nearer to an oasis. She saw a big drilling rig, most likely boring test wells, and beyond that, extensive salt pans. The ridge descended sharply to join the main road again. It pointed straight across the level landscape, heading to the northeast and the coast beyond.

Heading to Barawe.

Heading to Joyce.

Bashir turned to her. "Welcome to Somalia."

Chapter Eighteen

Pope waited for Lieutenant Commander McMahon outside the ship's mess. The SEALs were inside, running through their final briefing, and it was not lost on Pope that he hadn't been invited to participate. *Fair enough,* he thought. He wouldn't have invited outsiders into one of his briefings either. You never really knew who you were dealing with. Better not to take chances.

They finished and the men filed out. They all looked like typical, average SEALs: around six foot tall, lean physiques, buzz-cut hair.

McMahon was the last outside. "Captain Pope," he said. "Will you walk with me?"

They went out onto the flight deck. The Knighthawk that Pope had arrived in had been lashed to its bindings and, as they watched, an Osprey was coming in to land.

"When are your men going out?"

"Twenty-four hundred hours," he said. "Figure it's going to be an hour to get there, so we'll be looking at assaulting at zero one hundred hours."

"Any new intel?"

"No, Captain. Nothing I haven't told you about."

There was an awkward pause.

"Look, let's put our cards on the table, alright? I'm getting the feeling that we're not sharing all the information that we have here."

"Go ahead."

"All I know is that four of the hostages over there"—he gestured out towards the horizon—"have British passports. And that's why you're here. We're working together, right? Cooperating. That sound about right to you?"

"It does."

"And we also know that you're saying you've got an asset in the town. Right?"

"Possibly."

He raised an eyebrow at the equivocation. "*Possibly?*"

Pope knew he should follow the script, but he also knew that if he didn't give the lieutenant commander a little additional information, then it would make things much more dangerous for Beatrix once things started to heat up.

"Between us, we may have an ex-operative there. I left her in Kenya before the chopper came to bring me out here. She had transport, and she was heading east. I don't know if she was able to get across the border or not."

"Hold on. She?"

"Yes. And she's on her own. No support from us. And so far beyond deniable that it isn't true. As far as we're concerned, she doesn't exist."

"Okay." The lieutenant commander looked perplexed. "So you haven't been in touch with her since?"

"Why would I? Technically, she doesn't work for us anymore."

"She's a free agent?"

"Precisely."

"And you can't tell me anything else?"

Pope shook his head. "There's nothing else to tell."

"Not where she might be? What she might do?"

Pope wanted to be honest and tell the lieutenant commander that Beatrix was going to mount her own attack under the cover of the SEALs' assault, but that was a step too far. He dared not. Stone was right about that. There was a good chance that a wild card like that would mean the SEALs aborted the mission. And he doubted whether that would stop Beatrix from going in. She would do it solo, and that would be as good as a suicide mission, no matter how good she was or might once have been. He balanced up the merits of speaking and staying silent and decided, however perverse, that she stood a better chance of survival if he remained vague.

"You don't need to worry," he said. "She won't get in your way. I doubt you'll even know she's there."

"I got to be honest with you, Pope, that's not going to do her much good once the bullets start to fly. If she's there and she does get involved, we won't be able to discriminate. She'll probably get shot. If she doesn't get shot, and she gets compromised, we won't be able to stop and get her out. This is all focussed on the hostages."

Pope nodded. "I understand. And you're being very reasonable. If I could tell you more, I would."

Chapter Nineteen

ashir drove on. He followed the *panya* until it fed, quite brazenly, onto a road that led east to Jilib and then Barawe. The landscape was flat and arid, and the midday heat was punishing. The road eventually turned due east, and they followed it as it then bent to the north. They continued through a belt of junipers towards Jilib.

"Third largest city in Somalia," Bashir said. "Mogadishu is largest, then Hargesia, in the north."

They crested a shallow rise before the gradual depression into where the city was set. It spread out all the way to the hazy horizon. It had been levelled during the civil war, and the buildings that had replaced it tended to be lower-slung, with a handful of high-rises starting to appear in the centre of town.

"We're going through it?"

"I deliver the water here. You should stay in the truck."

"Pull over."

He did as she asked. She reached into her bag for the niqāb and jilbāb that she had bought at the airport before they left Morocco. She went around the truck so that Bashir could not see her, pulled the cloak over her head and then pulled and tugged it until it fell naturally around her. The veil was next, and she arranged it around her face until it fell comfortably. She looked into the wing mirror: only her eyes were visible. She strapped on her shoulder holster. The garments served an even more useful purpose than obscuring her identity. It would be more difficult to identify her as a Westerner now, and she would be able to wear her semi-automatic with no fear of it being discovered.

It took a moment to adjust to having the surprisingly thick material over her mouth, and her field of vision restricted. Finally satisfied, she turned to Bashir.

"Very good," he said.

"Can you see who I am?"

"Impossible to say."

"Good."

"What is this? Journalist's trick?"

"Something like that."

She indicated that Bashir should proceed, and he drove into the city, merging with the steady stream of traffic that had started to accumulate on the approach. They passed into the city limits, passing half a dozen mosques and a hospital. The town was a surprise. It was big and blowsy, a metropolis that would not have looked out of place in some of Somalia's more affluent neighbourhoods. It had recovered miraculously well from the war, the only obvious relic of which was the Soviet-era MiG in Somali air force colours that had been shot down in the act of strafing the city, now restored and mounted on a plinth in the middle of a roundabout.

The man who was buying Bashir's water was waiting for them in a truck near the entrance to a large covered market, the East African equivalent of a Moroccan souk. Beatrix saw a shoe stall, the teetering stacks smelling of plastic and fresh leather; there was a sari shop, the bolts of colour like garish lures to tempt customers inside;

stalls piled high with oranges and lemons, both of which were prolific nearer to the coast.

Bashir reversed the truck so that the crates of water could be thrown from one vehicle into the other and clambered up into the back.

"You want some food?" Beatrix asked him.

"Sure."

There was a refreshments stall at the entrance to the market. She approached the stall, pointed to a stack of triangular *sabmuusas*, and then held up five fingers. They could have two now, and the others would serve as rations for later.

"Four shillings," the man replied in guttural Arabic, and Beatrix handed him the money.

He put the food into a bag and handed it to her. She dipped her head, feeling the weight of the Glock 17 underneath her arm.

She strolled into the market and soaked in the sights and sounds. There were children, practically feral, scurrying between the stalls. Goats wandered wherever they wanted. The buildings were ramshackle, tarpaulins replacing shattered roofs in many places. Traders sold wicker baskets, fruit, vegetables. She turned a corner into a narrow passageway where it was only possible to walk in single file. Dust was everywhere, heavy and cloying, and the heat from the sun was dizzying.

She turned around and retraced her steps back to the truck.

Bashir had finished and was wiping his face with a towel.

"Very hot work," he said.

"Here." She handed him one of the *sabmuusas*.

"Very good," he said, biting down.

She ate hers, too. It was ground fish spiced with hot green pepper, the pastry thin and crispy.

"How far from here?" she said when they had finished.

"One hundred seventy-five kilometres. We will be there in four hours."

Chapter Twenty

They were a short distance to the north of Jilib when a sudden juddering came from the left-hand side of the truck. Bashir struggled to maintain control before the juddering abruptly worsened. They heard a repeated slap slap slap from outside. He freewheeled over to the side of the road and parked on the rough strip of rocky scrub between the asphalt and the sand.

Beatrix opened the door and jumped down to the ground. The rear tyre on her side of the truck was flat.

"Damn it," Bashir said.

"Do you have a spare?"

"Yes."

"And a jack?"

"Of course."

"So, it's not a problem. We change it."

She found a couple of decent-sized rocks from the side of the road and used them as chocks to stop the front and back wheels. Bashir rolled a spare out of the back of the truck and dropped a jack after it. Beatrix took off the niqāb and jilbāb and set to work, sliding under the truck and positioning the jack on the beam of the frame just behind the front of the rear wheel. She raised the jack until it was supporting the truck.

Bashir was standing next to her, watching. "You want a hand?" he asked, evidently embarrassed to be rendered redundant, especially by a woman.

"Don't worry. I've got it."

"It would be better if I did it. It would not be good for you to be seen."

"I'll be quicker than you," she said.

He fussed around nervously as she set to it.

"How far are we from Barawe?" she asked.

"Thirty miles."

"How much further can you take me?"

"I take you to the outskirts. Maybe two miles from the town. Is that alright?"

"Works for me."

She loosened the lug nuts, jacked the truck properly off the ground, kicked the wheel until it fell off and then placed the spare on the hub. She was about to replace the lug nuts when Bashir cursed colourfully.

She stood up and straightened her back, shielding her eyes as she looked back down the road to Jilib.

An old black Nissan flatbed pickup truck was climbing the coast road towards them. As it drew nearer, she saw that it was what they called a "Technical," a Toyota Hilux with a big Russian 12.7mm calibre DShK machine gun mounted in the back. There was a driver, a passenger next to him and six masked men in the back, legs hanging over the sides, their flip-flops dangling. They all had AK-47s.

"It is an al-Shabaab patrol," Bashir said.

"What will they do?"

"They will ask what we are doing."

"And?"

"And I will say I have come from Dadaab to make a collection in Barawe."

"And they'll believe that?"

"We must hope so. Please, you must get in the truck. Shut the door. We must hope they have not seen you."

Beatrix made a reflex assessment of the situation. They were a minute away. They must have seen her by now. She certainly did not have time to finish off fitting the new wheel so that they might make an escape. Even if there was time, the Technical was faster than the battered old truck and the 12.7mm machine gun would make short work of it. The desert was bleak and empty on either side, and if she ran to the west, she would be cut off by the sea before she had covered a kilometre. No. A tactical withdrawal was impossible. They were going to have to face them.

She pulled herself into the cab and shut the door. She checked in the mirror that the veil of the niqāb was covering her eyes.

She watched as the Nissan slowed and drew onto the side of the road twenty feet behind them. Bashir waited for them. One of the men in the back jumped down and came towards him. He was wearing a *ma'awii*, a sarong-style skirt, and two bandoliers of cased cartridges crossed over his chest. His face was covered with a red-and-white-chequered *kufiya*. The other men in the back of the truck were dressed similarly.

Beatrix could hear the conversation through the open window.

"What are you doing?"

"I have a flat tyre, brother."

The man rested the stock of his AK on the sandy asphalt, his hand around the barrel. "Where are you going?"

"Barawe."

"What for?" His Arabic was halting. He was not a native Somali.

"I make a collection there."

"Of what?"

"Fruit, brother."

"And then?"

"Back to Dabaab. The camps."

"You have a woman with you."

Bashir hesitated. "Yes. She is in the truck."

"Who is she? Your wife?"

"No . . ."

"Tell her to come here."

"She is tired. We have had a long . . ."

His voice tightened with anger. "Tell her to come here."

Beatrix opened the door and jumped down to the road.

"Assalamu alaykum," the man said. "Peace be upon you."

Beatrix's Arabic was better than his: *"Wa alaykum us salaam."* "And peace also be with you."

"You were changing the wheel."

"Yes, brother."

"That is not a job for a woman."

"Two people are quicker than one."

"It is not a job for a woman." He turned to Bashir. "She should not be outside the house. It is an offence."

"I am sorry," she said.

She saw the man's eyes narrow with suspicion. "What is your name?" he asked her.

Beatrix thought fast. "Fatima." It was the name of Mohammed's wife.

"And where do you live?"

"I live in Dadaab."

She saw a glint of cunning in his eyes. A predator trapping his prey. "Where in Dadaab do you live? Where exactly? Which street?"

Beatrix recalled the maps she had studied. "Jidka Barawe," she said. "Near Barka Shaqaalaha. The restaurant. Do you know it?"

He paused, the wrinkles around his eyes suggesting a frown. "You must come with us."

"Why?"

"Because you should not be out on the road like this. It is an offence!"

Beatrix felt the adrenaline spiking her veins.

Bashir was backing away.

"You," the man said, pointing at him. "Stay there." He turned, put his fingers to his lips and whistled. "I need two of you," he called out. "And bring the lash." Two men dropped down from the flatbed and slouched across to them.

"Please," Bashir said.

The first man turned to the newcomers. "This dog has brought this woman from Dadaab. What do you think of that?"

One of the men pulled the *kufiya* away from his mouth and spat on the ground. He had a coil of rope with him.

"Hold him," the first man said. "He must be whipped."

The men each took an arm and grabbed. Bashir was too terrified to move.

The first man approached Beatrix until he was oppressively close to her. She stepped back. He came forward again until he had penned her against the back of the truck.

"I think she is lying to us," he said to the others. "You are not from Dadaab. I do not believe you."

"It is true."

Last chance, she thought. *One more step.*

"I think perhaps she needs to be whipped, too."

"I agree," one of the new men said, his leer obvious even behind the scarf.

Beatrix's hand was hidden by the folds of the gown. "Please, brother."

The first man reached a hand for the veil, and as his fingers closed around the fabric and moved it aside, he saw her flinty eyes. It was the last thing he would ever see. Beatrix's hand struck out from the folds of the niqāb, her *kukri* gripped tight in her fist. The blade sliced across his throat, opening it from the point of the left clavicle all the way in a diagonal line to the side of his throat below his right ear. His eyes bulged at the impossible, horrible unexpectedness, his lifeblood spurting out for every dying beat of his heart.

The fighter to the left of Bashir dropped his AK into the grit and sand, his eyes wide with terror.

Beatrix allowed the upwards momentum of her first stroke to abate and then slashed back down again, spinning the grip in her palm so that the tip of the curved blade was pointing back down again, the smooth stroke terminating between the second man's ribs, the blade puncturing his heart.

The third man turned and ran back towards the truck.

Beatrix muscled the *kukri* out of the torso of her second victim and, aiming and flinging the knife as she dropped down to her knee, sent it at him in an unerring course that ended with the blade buried up to the handle between his shoulders.

Bashir gibbered in terror.

She reached down for the fallen AK and a spare magazine, flicked the selector to automatic and fired in controlled volleys as she walked to the pickup. The windshield went milky white as it spiderwebbed and then, immediately afterwards, splashed vivid red from the inside as the driver and passenger were peppered by the barrage.

The magazine went dry. Beatrix pressed the catch to eject it, canted the fresh magazine forward so that the lug on the front engaged with the recess in the magazine wall, then pulled it back sharply until it snapped into place.

The three men in the flatbed vaulted the gate and ran.

Beatrix zeroed in on the man to the left and fired.

Two bullets thudded into his back.

She switched to the man in the middle.

A bullet severed his spinal cord between the fourth and fifth vertebrae. He dropped, paralysed.

The third man was fifty feet away and running hard. Beatrix pressed the stock into her shoulder, zeroed the front and back sights, and squeezed off a final three-round burst.

Two shots missed. The third blew his skull apart like a rotten cantaloupe.

Eight men.

All dead.

Less than twenty seconds.

The man she had paralysed was moaning incoherently. She was on the way to the pickup and so she charitably put a round into his head.

She tore the *kufiya* from one of the men and used it to clean the blood from her knife. She dropped the soiled garment into the flatbed.

She scavenged three full magazines from the dead bodies and returned to the truck.

Bashir was on his knees.

"I'm not going to insist you take me into Barawe," she said, "but you need to get me closer than this. Like we agreed. Alright?" He was shaking. "Come on, Bashir. Get up."

"You are not a journalist."

"No. I'm not. Get up, Bashir, or I'll take the truck and leave you here."

She went back to the wheel, took up the wrench and started to tighten the nuts.

Chapter Twenty-One

We can't just wait and do nothing," Joe said.

They had moved to the far side of the room, leaving two men near the door so that they could hear if anyone approached down the stairs.

"We're not going to."

"So what are we going to do?" Harry Torres retorted angrily.

Joyce and the three other men from Manage Risk had become much less self-assured and much more defensive. It must have been obvious to them that they were relying on the sufferance of the others now.

"I don't know," Joe admitted.

"You want to know the way I see it?" Torres asked. "We should give them what they want. Maybe that will mean the rest of us can live."

"We're not doing that," Joe said. "We talked about that."

"And they keep killing us."

"Pretty fucking poorly!" Barry Miller said with sudden heat.

Joyce got up and came over. The others followed behind him.

"About time," Miller said. "You better have an idea to get us out of this."

"I told the captain. We're in a bad situation. There's no easy way out of this."

"So, what? You want us to do what? Wait?"

"That's our best option."

Torres gaped. "Are you *serious*?"

"There's nothing we can do down here. We would all be killed."

"I don't know if you've noticed, but we're like cattle waiting for the slaughter here."

"We won't have to wait much longer. You want to know what's happening outside? Two things. Your government knows where we are. The first thing, they'll have drones overhead right now. High up, invisible, but they'll be getting real-time video and intel. They might have a satellite, too. They'll know where we are, how many men they have, their defensive posture, everything. The second thing, they'll have men ready to come in and get us out. Could be Delta, could be the SAS. They'll be close now. They'll have been flown into theatre overnight. Maybe they jumped into the sea and got picked up by a frigate. Maybe they're in Kenya or Ethiopia, ready to get on board a Hercules now. But close. And when they get here, they are going to chew these fishermen up like you wouldn't believe. *That's* when we make our move. That's when we get out."

"That's all very interesting," Torres said, "but you're guessing. You don't know any of that. Maybe they don't know where we are. Maybe they decide this place is impossible to attack. Fuck, maybe they just drop a bomb and take all of us out together."

The other men sounded their agreement.

"That's not how it's going to happen," Joyce said.

"Look, I don't like to say it, really I don't, but we've got another card to play. We can say it was you who took out the boy on the boat."

"And they'll kill us."

"We're all dead anyway."

Joyce looked at Torres hard and cold. "You're not telling them anything."

"You going to try and stop me?"

Torres had a reputation as a bit of a firebrand.

"Harry . . ." Joe said.

Before Joe could tell him to stand down, he had taken a step towards Joyce and squared up.

"Harry . . ."

Joyce flashed his left hand towards Torres's face in a feint, Torres raised his hands to block, Joyce sidestepped him and hooked his right arm around his throat. He took a quarter turn and squeezed, choking Torres and then forcing him to his knees. Joe stepped forward, but he was blocked off by McGuinness, the number two Manage Risk man. The other men got to their feet, but Bloom and Anderton stepped into their way.

Torres started to gasp, his eyes bulged and his lips began to turn blue. Joyce maintained the grip, maybe even tightened it.

Joe tried to get around McGuinness. "You're choking him!"

He jostled up against him, and the Ulsterman responded by driving his fist into his gut. He dropped to his knees, winded.

Joyce kept squeezing.

Barry Miller rushed the other two men, but they repelled him with embarrassing ease.

Joyce released Torres, and he dropped to the floor of the basement. He didn't move.

Joe crawled forward and pushed him onto his back. His eyes had rolled up, just the whites showing. He felt for a pulse. There was none.

"Shit," he said, opening Torres's mouth, pinching his nose and bending so that he could breathe into him.

One. Two. Three.

He leaned back, lacing his fingers and placing his hands over his heart. He pumped, regular, fifteen times.

"Come on," he begged. "Come on."

Joyce stood back and watched.

Joe repeated the routine two more times, but Torres did not respond.

"You killed him," he said, gasping.

"If anyone says anything to them about who we are, you won't have to worry about what might happen to you outside. *We'll* kill you. All of you." He turned his gaze on Joe. "Do you understand, Captain?"

Chapter Twenty-Two

The town of Barawe came into view as the highway continued to the north. They were a mile away. Bashir pulled over to the scrub at the side of the asphalt, and Beatrix took out her field glasses. She scoped the town from north to south.

Bashir had given her a little history on the drive north. Barawe was an ancient settlement, and tradition said that the pioneer settlers built their town between "the red dunes" and "the white sands." It was set around a crescent bay, shielded by a spit of land that was furnished with a sixteenth-century Portuguese lighthouse. The town comprised a series of whitewashed coral buildings that extended back for a mile from the water's edge. The streets were wider than those in the other settlements they had passed, and the windows, so often narrow, were wide and inviting. She saw a number of bridges that extended across the street from the roof of one house to the roof of its neighbour. The sand on the beach was white, and the sea was bright blue. The town made its meagre income through the trade of charcoal, and Beatrix could make out a series of jetties and the dirty boats that would transport the fuel to its destination. There were skiffs on the beach and plenty of men working around them.

Bashir had been quiet after what had happened earlier. He looked at her completely differently. Before, she could tell that he had considered her a foolish westerner who didn't understand the risks that would be attendant upon her trip into the country. A cosseted, pampered journalist who would come to realise that the story was not as important as she thought it was. Now, though, he had changed his mind. She had no idea what he must think of her now, but whatever it was, it had frightened him into silence. She had spent the rest of the drive north cleaning and then sharpening the blade of the *kukri*. Bashir very conspicuously kept his eyes on the road.

She took the photographs from the drone and spread them out on the dash, trying to identify the house in which the hostages were being held. She found it as the light finally died: a three-storey house a couple of hundred feet from the beach, separated from the water by streets of smaller houses. If the SEALs were coming in from the sea, they were going to have to be stealthy or they would be fighting their way west through a reasonably built-up area.

Beatrix didn't like their chances.

"Is this close enough?"

"Wait until it's properly dark, then take me another half a mile closer. Don't worry. If anyone threatens us, I'll take them out."

"Yes," he said, even though it was obvious that the only thing he wanted to do was to turn around and set off back to the border.

They waited at the side of the road for another thirty minutes, watching as a handful of lights flickered on in the windows of the buildings. There was no municipal lighting, and the streets remained gloomy, thick pockets of dark into which she would be able to slide unseen. That was good. It would be easier to infiltrate without detection.

She turned the glasses to the uninhabited lighthouse and then out to sea. She could see nothing to suggest that an attack was imminent. She guessed that the SEALs would arrive aboard a warship and then make land aboard faster boats. But if that was right, there was no sign of anything. But that wasn't surprising. The ship would drift in with its running lights off. It would be difficult to make anything out from shore.

It might not be tonight either.

"Go on," she said. "A little closer and then you can leave me."

He started the engine and put the truck into first.

"How will you get out again?" he asked as they bumped onto the road.

"I'll have to improvise that," she said. "Don't worry. This won't be the first time."

Midnight.

Beatrix stood at the side of the road and watched as the tail lights of Bashir's truck winked out. She had paid him the money that they had agreed on and that was that. He had turned around and set off immediately.

She opened her rucksack and took out the black jacket and trousers. She changed at the side of the road, stuffing the niqāb into the bag, and then pulled on her combat boots. She took out a tub of camo paint and daubed it across her face, tied her hair back into a ponytail and then put on her gloves. She wouldn't be able to go about town in the daylight without the veil, but it would do her no good now. She would not be able to answer even the most basic question as to why she was on the street after midnight, and so she decided she would rather be completely mobile and unencumbered. She pulled on her riggers belt and the assortment of pouches and checked, for the final time, that she had her grenades, throwing knives and all the spare ammunition that she might need. She checked the retention strap that held her Glock in its holster, ducked her head through the sling of the Heckler & Koch MP-5 and settled it over her shoulders.

She was on the northern edge of the town. She set off, following Wadada Marka iyo Afgooye until its junction with Barawa Road, and approached the town from the northwest. The road swung crazily between the hills until it became the Jidka Baraawe and started to pass through the outskirts of the town. The scattered buildings amid the red sand became more frequent and then began to be grouped in blocks with smaller roads leading off left and right. The streets were quiet, but not deserted. She occasionally saw people in the doorways of the buildings and skirted them to remain unseen. She saw a group of young men wearing *ma'awiis*, the sarong-style skirt that the bandits on the road had been wearing. They were chewing *khat* and listening to music, and they didn't notice her as she ghosted by to the west.

Beatrix relied on her memory of the drone photographs, following the main road towards the sea. The house was fifty feet to the northwest of the mosque, and as the smell of salt grew stronger and stronger in her nostrils, she saw the minaret rise above the buildings.

Beatrix kept to the shadows and paused as she saw a man in the doorway of a building fifty feet ahead of her. He stopped, wrapped a turban around his head and neck and then set off in the direction of the mosque. She turned off the main road into an alley, running low and fast, jumping over a trash can and then avoiding the stray goat who had tipped it over.

She stopped at the exit of the alley and checked the main street as it cut across it from north to south.

She navigated against the minaret of the mosque until she was confident she was in line with the back of the house. The alley was hemmed in by eight-foot concrete walls on both sides, and there was an industrial bin half-blocking the way ahead. She planted her hands on the top and pushed off, vaulted onto the lid and then reached for the lip of the wall.

She scrambled up and looked over at the compound beyond.

The building was bigger than its neighbours and was surrounded by the concrete wall on all four sides, with a gate in the front. The wall was crumbling in places. There were no lights anywhere in the compound, and it was perfectly dark. As she watched, a *mujahideen* armed with an AK-47 made a lazy stroll around the perimeter of the building, the glowing red tip of his cigarette giving his location away. Beatrix held her breath, although she knew that there was no way that he would be able to see her. He loitered around the back, finishing his cigarette, and then tossed the dog end into the yard. It flashed sparks as it landed in the sand and gravel. The man knocked two times on a side door that Beatrix hadn't noticed. The door opened, a long finger of illumination from the light inside reaching out into the compound. The fighter went inside; the door closed, and it was dark again.

Beatrix turned. Behind her, and facing the compound, was a building of similar size to the one across the way. She had noticed it when she was scouting the town earlier and had noted it as promising. Now she could see that it more than met her expectations. This building was derelict. There were no doors, the glass in the window frames was broken and slogans in Arabic had been daubed across the whitewashed coral walls.

She clambered over the fence, crossed a short yard treacherous with faeces from dogs, goats and other animals, went inside and climbed the staircase to the third floor. The wide double-aspect windows offered a good view of the compound, the beach and the buildings in between.

She settled in to wait.

Chapter Twenty-Three

The SEALs did not come that night. Beatrix waited for them until four and saw and heard nothing. She knew that they would assault the town only during darkness, and it was too close to dawn by then. She had taken a couple of morphine tablets to dull the ache in her bones, but now she had run out of them. She would have to white-knuckle it the rest of the way until she could find more.

She lay down and grabbed a few hours of sleep.

The sun was streaming through the broken windows when she awoke. She still had the *sabmuusas,* and so there was no need for food, not that she would have left her hideout for something as banal as hunger. But she wanted to scout in the daylight, and so she decided to venture into the town. She put the MP-5 into the rucksack and hid it under loose floorboards. She put on her veil and cloak and unclipped the retention strap for the holstered Glock.

She made her way carefully outside.

She walked east, away from the coast, and into the heart of the town. She passed huts and houses, an abattoir that smelled of blood, a smoking house that reeked of the fish that were being cured. There was a market in the centre of the town. It was not as big as the one in Jilib, but there were still two dozen stalls. A stand offered different T-shirts for sale, and next to that was another laden down with shoes and sandals. Other stalls offered silver and gold, random pieces of clothing and household items. Beatrix stopped to watch as a man bartered for a pair of fake Ray-Bans and a belt. The trader settled for six thousand shillings, just less than a dollar. Further on, there were money exchangers with bundles of shillings wrapped in cling film that they would swap for dollars. Bags of local charcoal were stacked up in tall towers. A herd of camels was marched along the road that bounded the market to the abattoir. Mongooses darted between the tables, and a sea heron perched on a wall, looking down at the hectic scene below.

Every now and again she would see a young man with an AK-47, fighters from al-Shabaab who had come up from their houses by the beach.

She found a stall offering food. It was owned by a man with an orange beard and orange hair beneath his hat. The Quran forbade the use of black hair dye, and so many used brown henna which turned to orange in the sun. He had a large bowl of stew warming over an open charcoal fire and stacks of pancake-like bread called *canjeero* to be dipped into it. Beatrix bought a portion in a foil container and took it down to the beach. There was a quiet area one hundred yards from the house where the hostages were kept, and she sat on the sand, unclipping the fold of the veil that covered her mouth so that she could eat. It was early, but the temperature was already hot and getting hotter. The food tasted good. She finished it quickly, mopping up the residue with the *canjeero,* regretting that she had only bought one portion.

She stood and walked slowly in the direction of the house. She reached the area of the beach that was full of skiffs, the peaceful hushing of the tide interrupted by the scream of an angle grinder as an engine was repaired. She kept away from the men, and they paid her no heed.

She turned away from the sea and climbed towards the house. There were more fighters now, and she didn't want to push her luck. She got within fifty feet of the gate, memorising as much of the new detail as she could, and then turned away into a side alley and returned to the derelict property that way. She waited until she was sure that she was not observed and then hurried inside.

She stayed in the house for the rest of the day. She spent the time disassembling and then reassembling her Glock and then, when that was done, she switched her attention to the MP-5. She would not normally have disabled her weapons in a war zone, even for a brief time, but they had been exposed to a lot of dust and grit, and she did not want even the smallest chance of a misfire. She removed the magazine, inspected the chamber and the receiver, lifted off the bolt cover and took it to pieces. It took her an hour to clean it. The routine was reassuring, almost meditative, and she allowed her thoughts to drift.

She was counting on the SEALs. They would attack fast and stealthily, and when it started, it would be an excellent distraction from her own mission. They would come from the sea and make a frontal assault on the house, at least to start. She would move quickly, attack to the side, infiltrate, do what she had come to do and exfiltrate. She would slip in and out again like a ghost and leave before the SEALs even knew she was there.

That was the plan, of course. She knew well enough that plans tended not to stand up after the first contact had been made, but it was as good a place to start as any. She would adapt on the fly once things kicked off.

She thought of Joshua Joyce.

He was just a stone's throw away from her. Number Ten. Ex-SAS, one of the government's most dangerous assassins. He hadn't fired the shot that had killed her husband, but he had been in the house, and that made him equally complicit in her eyes. Equally guilty and equally deserving of her justice. He had rabbit-punched her from behind. He had kicked her while she was on the floor, slamming his boot into her ribs until she stopped moving, and made her promise that she would do whatever it was that they wanted her to do. She had shot him in the leg in the mêlée that followed, but that was just a down payment on the retribution that she was here to deliver. She raised her arm so that she could look at the fresh tattoo, the ink still vivid, almost luminous.

Johnny Ink had asked her whether she was still going to get the whole sleeve done.

Definitely.

Leave room for more.

Chapter Twenty-Four

Pope looked up. Here, out on the ocean, miles from land, there was little pollution to dim the stars, and they sparkled with an unusual brightness. There were millions of them, spread out across the vault of the heavens, and they cast plenty of light. The moon, too, was vivid. The illumination was not in Rose's favour. Far better for her if the sky was clouded. It might have bought her a small advantage, and the way Pope saw it, she was going to need all the advantages she could get.

The welldeck opened out at the stern of the ship, and there was an observation walkway that ran around the top of it. Pope made his way there and leaned against the railing directly above the churn of wash several metres below. The welldeck had been flooded with seawater, and the ramp had been lowered. The Mark V Special Operations Craft was loaded and ready to go. The SEALs were seated in the cabin, all eighteen of them, and the two assault craft that they would use to complete their trip to shore were tethered to the sloping deck of the SOC.

Lieutenant Commander McMahon joined him.

"You ever do anything like this?" he asked.

"Plenty of times."

"I still remember that feeling in the pit of my stomach."

"Adrenaline."

"If your asset is still in town, she wants to keep her head down. It's going to get interesting at"—he looked down at his watch—"about zero one hundred hours."

Pope agreed with the sentiment, but he knew that keeping out of the way was not in Beatrix Rose's nature.

The sailor on the walkway opposite Pope took a green flag and waved it.

The mooring lines were released, and the boat edged forward, passing through the aperture and bobbing down into the deeper water beyond. The senior chief petty officer looked up from the boat and raised his hand. McMahon returned the gesture. The big jets kicked in, and it jerked away sharply, carving quietly through the ocean.

Pope watched.

There they go.

No stopping it now.

———

She allowed herself to sleep. It would only be for a few hours, but her body badly needed it. She was expending too much energy fighting the cancer, and she was barely resting to recharge. When she finally awoke, it was much later. She blinked the sleep out of her eyes and looked at her watch.

Zero ten hours.

Shit.

She had been sleeping for too long.

Something had woken her.

A noise.

Chanting.

She pressed herself up against the wall and slowly moved across it so that she could look out the window.

There was activity at the front of the house. Beatrix watched from her hiding place as the main door was opened and a dozen armed men exited. The chanting got louder.

Allahu akbar.

Allahu akbar.

Allahu akbar.

They were dressed in similar fashion to the men she had taken down on the road outside Barawe. They had ammo belts and AKs and RPG-7s, red-and-white-chequered *kufiyas* hiding their faces. Beatrix counted fourteen of them.

Another man came out with a digital camera equipped with a powerful light. He went to the front of the group and took up position, making preparations for what Beatrix knew was about to happen. Three more men came outside, two dragging a third, struggling and protesting for all he was worth.

Beatrix hurriedly examined him through her field glasses.

It wasn't Joyce.

The man was hauled in front of the semi-circle and forced to his knees. He fought as hard as he could, and for a moment, it looked as if he was going to be too difficult to subdue, but then one of the group stepped forward and cold-cocked him in the back of the skull with the stock of his AK-47. The man's head jerked forward violently and then hung still.

She put the glasses down and traced her fingertips over the MP-5. The gun didn't have the range to be accurate from here. An excellent sniper rifle wouldn't have been much more helpful either. She would have been able to plug two or three of them before they got into cover, but she would betray her position and lose the element of surprise that was critical to the success of her mission. If she intervened now, there would be no way to get to Joyce. He would be lined up with the other hostages and shot.

That was unacceptable.

She picked up the glasses again. A man stepped before the camera. He was holding a long machete, its blade glittering darkly in the light from the camera. He started to speak.

"Praise be to Allah who created the creation for his worship and commanded them to be just and permitted the wronged one to retaliate against the oppressor in kind."

She turned away from the window. A single scream rose into the night, bracketed by fervent chanting to Allah.

She picked up her *kukri* and the whetstone and settled into a rhythmic stroke and counterstroke, sharpening the blade.

Two of the Manage Risk soldiers were watching at the ventilation bricks. Joe couldn't. He just couldn't. But he could hear Farax's words, his sermon, and that was enough.

"Peace be upon he who follows the Guidance. People of America, this demonstration is for you and concerns war and its causes and results. We fight because we are free men who don't sleep under oppression. We want to restore freedom to our nation. Just as you lay waste to the nations of Islam all around the world, so shall we lay waste to yours and to your people."

They had come down to the basement ten minutes earlier. Farax had seen Torres dead on the floor and asked what had happened. Joe had just shaken his head.

Farax must have known what had happened, but he did not take action. He wanted Joe to tell him. Why? Perhaps it was as simple as a battle of wills. The American captain, with his money and his influence, against a poor and pious holy man. Perhaps he wanted to see Joe crack. Perhaps he found a perverse sort of pleasure in the situation, putting a good man in a position where he had to choose between his morals and his survival. Was there pleasure in watching him as, slowly and incrementally, the instinct to survive took charge?

Farax had asked about the sniper again.

"I don't know which one it was," Joe said, looking at the floor. He raised his arm and pointed, still looking down. "But those are the soldiers. One of them."

Joyce had cursed at him, but there was nothing he could do. Farax called up the stairs, and another two men appeared, each of them armed with an AK. There were four of them now, and they raised their rifles at the Manage Risk operatives and penned them at the far side of the room, away from the others.

"These men will stay with you now," Farax had explained. He had pointed at Torres's body. "This must not happen again."

"That's what you wanted," Joe said to him. "Right? Can we go now?" he begged. He had almost fallen to his knees. He knew how pitiful he sounded.

Farax beamed a big, white smile and clapped Joe on the shoulder. He looked into his face and told him that he had done the right thing but that he should have done so earlier, when he had asked him for the first time, and maybe none of this would have been necessary.

He reached out to rest a hand against Joe's cheek and then took it away to point at Barry Miller.

"Him."

And now Joe closed his eyes, but he couldn't shut out Farax's voice:

"No one except a dumb thief plays with the security of others and then makes himself believe he will be secure. Whereas thinking people, when disaster strikes, make it their priority to look for its causes in order to prevent it from happening again."

Miller had struggled, but he had been overpowered. Two of the fighters had dragged him outside. Three had stayed: two had aimed their rifles at the soldiers, and the other one had covered the crew.

"Your security is in your own hands. And every state that doesn't play with our security has automatically guaranteed its own security. And Allah is our Guardian and Helper, while you have no Guardian or Helper. All peace be upon he who follows the Guidance."

No one was going to move.

The resistance had been beaten out of them.

Chapter Twenty-Five

It was just after two in the morning when Beatrix finally knew that they were coming. They were approaching the beach, lights out, and it was the engines that she heard first. A high-pitched whine that lowered in frequency as it drew nearer and then became recognisable as two powerful diesel engines. She scanned the water with the night vision glasses until she found them: rigid inflatables with outboard motors, coming in fast. They would have started the mission aboard a warship and then transported from that ship to closer in aboard a bigger Mark V that would now be waiting for them out in deeper water. Each raiding craft looked to be around five metres from bow to stern, and she counted nine men on each. Eighteen men in total. That was in line with Pope's intelligence. They were sending a whole platoon to get the job done.

It was a stealthy infiltration, but now it was going to get hot, and quickly.

The beach was deserted. The two boats raced up and slid onto the sand. The platoon vaulted onto the beach, moving with the assuredness of men who had conducted infiltrations like this many times before. They split into two units of nine men each, approaching the compound through the streets from the east and the southeast.

Beatrix had an excellent view.

The men moved low to the ground and fast, with bulky silhouettes due to the heavy bags they were carrying. They ranged in front of the building in overlapping arcs, moving silently, communicating with hand signals.

She caught a flash of light in the corner of her eye. She looked at the house. The guard she had seen yesterday was outside again, holding a flame to the cigarette that was clasped between his lips.

Bad timing, she thought.

He strolled around to the front of the house, right in front of the SEALs.

One of the Americans was hiding behind a waist-high wall. The *mujahideen* was on the other side of the wall, less than a couple of feet away from him.

She held her breath.

They held their fire.

The man turned and wandered slowly back around to the rear door, dropping the cigarette.

He had only smoked half of it.

He had seen them. He was bluffing them.

Hand signals from the SEALs.

Two of them advanced.

She heard a shout, close, from the house, and then the first rattle of gunfire.

Now.

The first volley merged with another and then another. The fighters were firing out of the ground and first floor windows with AKs and semi-automatics. It was impossible to say how many of them were still inside, but there had to be at least a dozen.

The two SEALs in the vanguard dived into cover. The others were taking heavy fire, too, and, as she watched and assessed, they returned fire even as they retreated into a more defensive alignment.

Now.

She shrugged the rucksack over her shoulders, ran down the stairs, vaulted the fence and then the wall, and dropped down into the compound beyond.

Joe heard the clatter of gunfire from the floor above them. The expression on the face of the three guards changed from surly confidence to confusion and then fright.

McGuinness went to the ventilation bricks and tried to look out.

"Back!" one of the guards yelled, waving his rifle. "Back!"

"What is it?" Joyce asked.

"The cavalry."

Joyce pushed himself to his feet and rolled his shoulders. He turned to the guards. "Things are about to get interesting for you."

If they understood his English, they didn't show it.

"Back!"

The guards were panicking. They jabbed the AKs towards them, shouting at Joyce and McGuinness incomprehensibly.

Joe watched as one of the other men, Bloom, edged away from the wall, opening up the group so that it was more difficult to cover all four of them.

"Sit down, Joyce!" Joe shouted. "They'll shoot us!"

The guard watching over them shouted at him to be quiet.

None of the guards had covered Bloom.

"What are you going to do, boys?" Joyce taunted. "You know who that is? My guess is that's Uncle Sam. It'll be a full SEAL team with a full combat load. Hell, boys, it's one of the most violent things man has ever created."

"Quiet! Back, back!"

"My guess, you've got a few minutes left to live." Joyce mimed that they should lay their rifles down. "You put them down, and maybe I can help you."

Bloom kept moving, trying to flank them.

McGuiness took a step forward.

"Stop! You, back!"

They were distracting them.

A big risk.

"You, back!"

Joe closed his eyes.

Gunshots.

———⌣———

One of the *mujahideen* emerged from the back entrance, fumbling a magazine into his AK. He was going to try and flank the SEALs.

Beatrix saw him a half second before he saw her.

That was enough.

She let her MP-5 hang from its sling, her right hand darting to the bandolier of throwing knives that double-crossed her chest, taking one out and flinging it before the fighter had even started to bring his rifle around. The knife was double-edged and weighed around ninety grams. It flashed across the yard in a streak of silver, its trajectory terminating in the man's throat. His carotid artery was severed, the blood that sprayed out into the yard almost black in the dark light. He pawed at the foreign object that had miraculously lodged in his neck, stumbling out from the shelter of the building.

Beatrix intercepted him quickly, her left arm looping around his chest and her right unsheathing her *kukri* and stabbing him in the heart. She dropped the body in the shadows.

She gripped the forestock of the MP-5 with her left hand, her right resting so that her finger was curled lightly around the trigger, and pushed the door open with her foot.

She saw a young man in a state of undress, pulling a robe over his head, his rifle propped against the wall beside him. She fired a three-shot burst and took him out while he was still struggling with the robe. There was a terrific clamour of automatic gunfire from the rooms to her right, and she hoped that her contribution to it might go unnoticed.

She was in a corridor that looked as if it ran the length of the building. She assessed it: three doors right, two doors left, an open door before a flight of stairs going down. She had no idea on which floor the hostages were being held, but if it were her, she would choose the one that was easier to secure and defend.

A cellar, perhaps.

She heard the sound of exploding grenades. She couldn't tell if they had been thrown by the *mujahideen* or the SEALs.

She had to be quick.

If the SEALs fell back, she would be outnumbered by the *mujahideen*.

If the SEALs stormed the house, she would lose her moment with Joyce.

Quick.

She hurried to the stairs. She descended.

She reached a second door.

Wooden. Solid. Locked.

A key hung from a hook on the wall, and when she tried it, the lock turned.

The basement had been turned into a large cell. It was windowless and damp, with no light save the glow that leeched in from the open door and a little from ventilation bricks below the ceiling.

There was a scene of chaotic, fluid confusion inside.

The prisoners were struggling with three Somalis. Four of the westerners were on the floor. They looked as if they had been shot, blood and brains on the floor and the wall. Two of them looked like soldiers. One of the Somalis had a deep wound in his shoulder.

Her eyes flashed over the room and assessed it.

She aimed and fired: once, twice, three times.

The Somalis went down, gut-shot, gaping wounds in their chests.

The hostages turned to face her.

Their faces showed confusion and then exultation.

Beatrix scanned them, ignored them.

She recognised one immediately.

She only had eyes for him.

His image had been burned into her memory.

"Hello, Number Ten."

He gaped in confusion. "How do you know . . ."

"You don't remember me?"

It dawned on him. "Jesus," he said. "Number One?"

Now he couldn't hide the fear in his eyes.

"Didn't think you'd see me again?"

"Not like this."

She glanced around. There was one other obvious soldier: stocky, short cropped hair. He was next to Joyce.

"Thank God," one of the bloodied men said, his voice cracked. "Are you getting us out?"

"Stay where you are," she snapped without looking at him.

She turned back to Joyce and walked closer.

"We don't have long. Where's Control?"

"I don't know."

She raised the MP-5 and aimed it. "*Where is he?*"

"I swear. I don't know."

"What *do* you know?"

"I heard he was on the run."

"Who told you that?"

"Duffy."

"You speak to him?"

"Now and again."

"And where is he?"

"I don't know for sure. We Skyped . . ."

The other man got up and took a step towards her. "Miss? We . . ."

Beatrix snapped at him. "Stay where you are."

She took another step towards Joyce.

The bloodied man said, "He killed my second mate."

"That right, Number Ten? Did you?"

Joyce stared hatred right through her.

"Where's Duffy?"

"Go to hell."

"Where's Duffy?"

"Fuck you."

Beatrix should have concentrated on the other men in the room, but she was tired and in pain and needed everything focussed on Joyce and his friend. She didn't notice that the bloodied man had moved next to her.

"You've got to get us out of here," he said.

He put his hand on her shoulder and tugged her around to face him.

A momentary distraction.

It was enough.

Joyce and the soldier took their chances.

They both rushed her.

They were close, too close for her to aim and shoot twice, and she wanted Joyce breathing for a moment yet.

Priorities.

She fired the MP-5 at the other man, taking off the top of his head. His legs skidded out from under him as he fell heavily on his back.

Joyce slammed into her, driving her back all the way across the cell.

He was twice Beatrix's weight and as strong as a bear.

They thudded against the wall, knocking the breath out of her. The MP-5 was pressed against her chest and made useless. He buried a punch into her gut, reached for her Glock and yanked it out of her holster.

He pulled the trigger just as she drove the heel of her hand into his face. The round missed her head by an inch, striking the wall and ricocheting away, stone chips drawing blood as they pinged into the nape of her neck.

Joyce fumbled the Glock and put his free hand to his face. His nose had been smashed, and blood was running down into his mouth. He staggered back away from her, blinded by pain.

Beatrix followed in and swept his legs out from under him, forcing him down onto his back. She dropped down and straddled his body, nailing him with a straight downward right to the head. He was pumped with adrenaline and her fist just bounced off his skull. His right hand scrabbled for the Glock on the floor behind him, found it. He swung it forward as she unsheathed her bloodied *kukri* and whipped it from left to right, a short and powerful swipe; the blade sliced through his wrist and severed it. Joyce's hand still held her Glock as it flopped down to the floor. The stump spouted blood and Joyce screamed.

She pressed the blade against the side of his throat.

"Last chance," Beatrix said with a dead-eyed intensity that could not possibly be mistaken. "Where is Duffy?"

Blood pumped out of the fleshy nub, but he had time yet. "He works for us," he said through a grimace of agony.

"Doing?"

"Bodyguard."

"What kind?"

"Executives. High rollers. Usual shit."

"Where?"

"Iraq."

"Thank you," she said.

She whipped the blade up and away, opening his throat. He pressed his remaining hand there, blood running through his fingers, and looked up at her as she knelt over him.

"Goodbye."

She raised the blade, clasped it in both hands, and drove it down.

⌣

Joe Thomas watched with wide, uncomprehending eyes. He had been sure she was part of the rescue attempt that was being mounted outside. Special Forces. He had thought she had come to get them out, and then he had watched as she had cold-bloodedly murdered Joyce and the other man. Now he didn't know what to think. There was a coldness in her eyes, a flat quality, as if the humanity had been smelted out of her. She was terrifying.

"Who are you?"

"I didn't come here for you. I came for him. And now I'm going. You should do the same."

"You need to help us. *Please*. We're not armed."

She gestured to the weaponry scattered on the floor. "Help yourself."

"Please," Joe pleaded with her. "*Please.* I have a family. A wife and children. Kids. We all have families. I'm not a soldier. None of us are. We wouldn't know the first thing."

The woman gritted her teeth. "Who are you?"

"I'm the captain."

"Damn it."

He pointed with a shaking hand at Joyce's body. "I don't know who you are or what it was between the two of you. I don't care what it was, but he was no friend of mine. I told you, he killed my second mate. He got what was coming to him. But you've got to help us. We're dead if you don't."

She paused, then exhaled.

"What's your name?"

"Joe Thomas."

"Alright, Joe. I'll help. Any of you got anything to say about what I just did?"

No one spoke.

"If you do anything stupid, you won't have to worry about them," she said, indicating the upper floors, "because I'll shoot you. We clear?"

"Yes," Joe answered for them.

"Take the AKs. Follow up behind me, close."

"What's going on up there?" Joe asked.

"A team of SEALs are going after the Somalis. They're not finding it as easy as they hoped."

"Can't we just make a run for it?"

"You need to get to the beach. You'd have to run right in front of the *mujahideen*. They'd cut you down. We're going to have to shoot our way out and hope the SEALs don't think we're on the other side."

"Alright," Joe said. "Anything else?"

"We need to hurry. If they don't think they can get to you, they're going to call down an airstrike. And I'd rather not be here when that happens."

Chapter Twenty-Six

T he body in the corridor had not been disturbed. It was face down, arms and legs flung wide, the robe bunched up around its shoulders and the halo of blood on the floor beginning to congeal.

The firing was continuing from the front rooms, the reports echoing into the corridor and muzzle flashes sparking like lightning strikes.

Beatrix took out two fresh magazines. She loaded the first and held the second in her left hand.

She held up a hand to indicate that the captain and his men should stay at the top of the stairs.

She pressed herself against the wall to the side of the open doorway.

She took an M67 fragmentation grenade from her rucksack and pulled the pin.

She released the spoon and started to count.

One thousand one.

She peeled into the doorway. Ten fighters. Some were at the windows, firing into the town beyond. Others were in cover, reloading or, in one case, trying to staunch the flow of blood from a gut shot. The injured man saw her, but it was too late by then.

One thousand three.

She rolled the grenade into the room and spun back into cover.

The six ounces of explosive detonated, a supercharged cloud of dust and debris billowing out of the doorway.

She spun back again and opened fire, fully automatic, swivelling at the hip as she sprayed lead into the room. The gun clattered, bouncing against her shoulder, a constant judder as she chewed through all thirty rounds in the magazine. When she was dry, she pirouetted back behind the doorway, reloaded, and then spun down and around and fired again.

There were no targets left when she was finished.

It was a massacre. The room stank of gunpowder, and sixty hot, copper-coated cases rolled around her feet.

The captain was behind her. "Where are the Americans?"

There was no sign of them. "They're falling back into the sea," she said.

"What about us?"

"They don't think they can get to you."

"But they can't just leave us!"

"We need to get to them. And we've got to hurry."

They sprinted into the yard. Fresh bullet holes had scarified the wall, and the gate was on the ground, blown off its hinges by breaching charges during the assault. They clambered over it. The street beyond was elevated, and Beatrix got a better view of the harbour. She saw it in the moonlight: the Mark V Special Operations Craft that would have transported the SEALs from the warship had come in closer to assist in their exfiltration. It was five hundred feet offshore now and like a mini destroyer: two 7.62mm Gatling guns, two .50 calibre machine guns and two 40mm grenade launchers. It was running parallel to the shore so that the weapons to port could fire, then it swung around so they could cool while the weapons to starboard took over.

The crew ran for it.

Beatrix paused.

She turned to the right and saw the alleyway that ran along the side of the compound. She could follow it, find a car and drive the hell out of town. The longer she stayed, the better the chance that she would cop a bullet, a lucky shot, or collapse from the pain that she was now barely able to ignore. She had been wired on adrenaline all night, and now the fatigue was setting in. Her bones throbbed with a deep ache, and her breathing was becoming ragged. The cancer was crippling her. She knew that she wouldn't be able to keep up the same pace for much longer.

She paused.

The captain stopped and turned, scurrying backwards. "Come on!" he yelled back at her. "*Run!*"

She saw a flash of movement from the hut just ahead of the captain. A fighter raised the barrel of an AK, and there would have been no prospect of him missing except for the throwing knife that tore across the space between them and ended up in the fleshy part of his bicep. A second knife ended its flight in the man's throat, and he toppled back into the hut.

The captain turned, saw the dying man and, realising how close he had been to death, stumbled and fell. Beatrix helped him up, and then, impelling him towards the rest of the crew, she brought up the rear.

What else could she do?

There came the chatter of automatic rifles as al-Shabaab fighters opened up on the beach. The Mark V's big Gatling guns laid down a curtain of brutal covering fire in response.

And then Beatrix saw it: a pencil-thin and yet blindingly bright blast of red light that was aimed behind them at the building.

She followed the red tracer to its origin. One of the SEALs was painting the building with a laser designator.

Oh *fuck*.

It was too dark to see anything, but she knew what was coming. A Reaper.

"*Incoming!*"

———

Farax had been sheltering on the first floor of the house. He had taken three men to the old bedrooms up there. The windows were narrow, almost like slits, and they had offered excellent protection when they opened up on the Americans. He and his men were well armed and determined. The Americans were frightening, but they would not take the house without bloodshed. Farax had heard tales of what had happened in Mogadishu all those years before. He knew that the Americans had no stomach for casualties. He was prepared to gamble that if they made it difficult enough, made it obvious that the cost of taking the house would be high, then they would baulk and retreat.

He swivelled into the window and emptied the magazine of his AK.

Damn. The Americans were not there.

They were retreating.

"Keep firing!" he yelled out. "They are falling back."

They were fighting them off.

Praise be to Allah!

They were doing it!

Farax glanced back through the window and saw the men sprinting away from the house. A woman followed behind them.

What?

It was the hostages. *His* hostages. The Americans must have freed them, and now they were trying to escape.

He turned back into the room.

"Give me that!" he shouted to one of the others. The man had just reloaded their RPG.

He hefted the launcher onto his shoulder and poked the grenade through the window. They were close, only fifty feet away. It was an easy shot. He couldn't miss from here.

His finger curled around the trigger.

He had started to squeeze it when he was momentarily blinded by a narrow beam of bright red light that shone across the front of the house. The intense red painted a pattern across his eyes, and he blinked to clear it away.

His vision returned just in time to see the object in the sky, carving through the air towards them.

Allahu akbar.

Allahu akbar.

Allahu . . .

⌣

The concussive blast wave from the explosion came first, picking Beatrix up and tossing her ten feet through the air, dropping her on her back onto gritty asphalt.

The second bomb detonated seconds after the first, and a huge fireball rolled outwards and over the top of her, singeing her clothes and her hair.

She rolled over and pressed herself up onto her hands and knees, dazed, the ringing in her ears the only noise that she could hear.

Other sounds gradually became audible: a man yelling out, hungry flames, collapsing masonry. She scrambled to her feet and turned. The house wasn't there any more. Three of the walls had been demolished, leaving the fourth still standing like a sick reminder of what a thousand pounds of high explosive could do. The rest of the structure had been obliterated as thoroughly as if a giant fist had smashed down onto it. The basement was exposed, and a thick pall of smoke was unfurling over the rousing town. A rushing, roaring burning crackled through the air.

Every al-Shabaab fighter in a ten-mile radius would be awake now.

The ringing in her ears continued. The blast like that, danger close, must have damaged both eardrums.

"We're missing two men," the captain yelled.

She checked quickly. He was right: two were gone.

"Too close to the blast. They're dead."

"What . . . I . . ."

"You've got to keep running."

"I can't just . . ."

She grabbed his wrist and yanked him. "Come on! Run!"

They sprinted again, following the road down to the sea.

A sudden wave of lethargy washed over her just as she jumped down from the concrete jetty to the beach below, and she stumbled and tripped, falling face first into the wet sand.

The captain stopped and dragged her to her knees. "Are you hurt?"

"Tripped," she said, although she had no breath and had to gasp the word out.

He hauled her upright. Her strength returned sufficiently for her to stand unaided, and she carried on, jogging with heavy legs towards the surf.

The SEALs had boarded the raiding craft and were gunning them hard towards the Mark V. The first boat skimmed across the surface and slid up the ramp that had been dropped at the stern.

The second was just behind it.

Beatrix aimed her MP-5 into the sky and emptied it.

"Hey!" the captain yelled, and he waved.

The others joined in. "Hey! Hey!"

They were spotted. A shout went up, the Mark V's engines flared and the boat swung around.

If the SEALs mistook them for tangos, they were finished. The Gatling guns would cut them to shreds.

But they didn't fire.

The second raiding craft changed course, curving around, its wake frothing behind it.

They were coming back for them.

Beatrix felt a moment of relief. "You're alright from here," she said.

"What do you mean?"

"They'll have you out in a couple of minutes."

"What?" He looked at her, baffled. "You're not coming?"

She had already thought about it. It would have been the easiest way to exfil, but the men had all seen her execute Joyce and the other man. There was no way she would be able to answer their questions without betraying her cause. The CIA would take her into custody. Pope would get her out, eventually, but how long would that take? A month? Two months? She was already dealing in months. She had an expiration date. She didn't have the luxury of spare time to squander on petty administration. There was still a lot for her to do.

"You'll be fine."

She was buffeted by another dizzying wave of fatigue and then, on its heels, a shiver of pain that almost brought her to her knees.

It was impossible to hide it.

"You've got to come with us."

"Good luck, Captain."

She turned her back on him and ran back into the town.

She found an old Soviet-era Lada. It was parked in a narrow alley beneath a sheet of orange tarpaulin. She opened the door, clashing it against the wall of the alley, and squeezed between it and the body of the vehicle until she was inside. She used the point of her *kukri* to snap off the plastic cover on the steering column. She thumbed through the harness connector for the wires that led to the battery, ignition and starter, then stripped away the insulation from the battery wires, and twisted them together. She sparked the starter wire to the battery wire, and the engine spluttered and turned over. She fed in revs until the engine was established.

She checked her watch: it was four in the morning.

She didn't want to be here when the sun came up.

It was way past time to go.

There had been activity in the town as she made her way to the vehicle. Armed fighters were gathering at the smoking remains of the house, warily looking seaward at the fast disappearing lights of the SEALs. That was in Beatrix's favour. They would not have expected any of the enemy to have remained behind, and they certainly would not have expected to find anyone heading inland, away from safety. She had moved in the darkness, breaking cover only when she was sure she was unobserved and then running as hard as she could until she was back in the embrace of the shadows again. Now she was trembling with exertion, and her clothes were soaked through with sweat.

She slapped the palm of her hand against the side of her head to try and clear the constant ringing, but it had no effect.

No time to worry about that.

She put the car into gear and rolled out onto the road.

She turned to the north and headed out of town.

Chapter Twenty-Seven

Beatrix drove quickly. It was much too early for traffic, but people were stirring. Some were at their windows or on the roofs of their buildings, looking towards the sea and the finger of thick grey smoke that was reaching into the darkened sky. Others were stumbling from their doorways, half dressed, roused by the thunderous blast. Some of them, the young men, had weapons. They looked askance at the old Lada as it raced by, bouncing across the uneven surface, all of them too slow to think of stopping it.

She thought she was going to make it until she turned the final corner onto the Barawa Road and saw the two Technicals reversing so that they were tailgate to tailgate, blocking the road. There were a dozen fighters there, all of them with AKs, and the two 12.7mm-calibre DShK machine guns were manned and aimed down the road towards her.

They were a hundred feet away.

Beatrix was closing at fifty miles an hour.

The machine guns opened fire, and tracers screamed out at her.

She weaved.

A round went through the windshield, throwing glass back into her face.

She yanked the wheel to the left, almost rolling the car as she sent it skidding and sliding off the road and onto the patch of rough that passed for the front yard of the huts that hemmed the road in. The machine guns kept firing, and she heard the *chunk-chunk-chunk* as three big rounds pulverised the bodywork, punching through the panels behind her and exploding through the seats.

The flying glass had sliced her face open.

The suspension shrieked in protest as she bounced over the rocky ground. She stamped on the brake, fishtailing the car as she aimed for the narrow space between the nearest two shacks. The side of the car slapped against one of them before the tyres found traction. She made it into the gap as the wooden boards detonated in a shower of splintered shards, another couple of rounds slamming into the rear of the car.

She felt warm blood on her lips.

The terrain behind the huts was rough, full of rocky outcrops and rutted sandy stretches. She could see the straight path of the Jilib road to her northwest, but even if she could pilot the Lada over the precarious ground, she knew that she wouldn't be able to outrun the Toyotas for very long. The sedan was horribly under-powered and in bad condition.

They would come after her, and there would be nothing that she could do about it.

Deal with that when you have to.

She was halfway to the road when she saw the first Technical, its lights scouring across the lightening darkness, bouncing along the road in her direction.

Half a mile away and closing fast.

She stamped on the gas as the second jeep appeared just behind the first.

The road was a couple of metres above the floor of the desert. Beatrix slalomed through a field of wheel-sized rocks and then buried the pedal. The Lada, protesting mightily, still picked up speed. She was doing forty as she ascended the slope, leaping into the air as she launched off the crest, slamming down onto the road. She hit the brakes and skidded through ninety degrees, pointing the car towards Jilib, then she hammered the gas again.

The car ticked quickly up to fifty.

The first Technical was five hundred feet behind her.

The machine gun roared out again.

⌣

The US Air Force had stationed an RQ-4 Global Hawk over eastern Somalia to monitor the operation. It was loitering at fifty thousand feet now, a little below its operational ceiling. The pilot was thousands of miles away in a bunker at Beale Air Force Base in California. His orders had been to stay over the town for the duration of the operation and to provide intelligence to the SEALs on the ground and to mission control on the *Tortuga*.

The Hawk had recorded everything: the SEALs' approach, the gun battle, the confusion in the aftermath. It had watched the SEALs falling back into the sea and what looked like a determined pursuit from the group of hostiles that had emerged from inside the house. Footage from the Hawk had been critical in green-lighting the order to destroy the house. It had watched as the two massive bombs pulverised it into brick dust and killed everyone inside.

The Hawk had watched as the survivors had transferred from the assault craft to the Mark V. It had watched as they started on their way to the *Tortuga* and safety. The operation, which had looked like it was going to be a catastrophic failure, was, instead, a partial success.

It turned out that what had looked like a pursuit was actually the escape of the hostages. The pilot didn't know how they had gotten away. Perhaps the SEALs had done enough.

Whatever the reason, the military had been lucky.

And the hostages had been even luckier.

Now the Hawk observed the three vehicles that were speeding out of Barawe. The pilot adjusted the track that the aircraft was following and focussed the cameras. He zoomed in: there was a sedan and two pickups. They were moving fast. As if they were trying to get away.

He called it in.

———⌣———

Beatrix pressed the gas all the way to the floor. The sedan was up to fifty-five, the engine struggling, the rev counter dangerously in the red. She doubted it would be able to maintain the same pace for long before the pistons were wrecked.

She glanced up in the mirror: the pickups were four hundred feet behind her and still gaining. They were going to reel her into range of their big guns and then tear her to pieces.

She gritted her teeth.

This wasn't how it was supposed to go down.

She saw the muzzle flash from the machine gun and heard the rapid thud-thud-thud as it fired. The remnants of the rear windshield exploded into the cabin, and rounds sliced through the air, some arcing through the left-hand side of the car and others passing harmlessly through the denuded front window.

Beatrix yanked the wheel to the right, popping onto two wheels for a moment as she swerved off the road. There was a sudden dip in the terrain, and the Lada lurched and then thumped down into it with a clang as the exhaust broke free, scraping a track through the sand and grit.

The manoeuvre put her out of reach of the big guns, but it allowed the pickups to close further.

It was a miracle that she hadn't been hit and an even bigger miracle that the car was still running.

Her luck couldn't last.

⌣

The pilot and sensor operator of the MQ-9 Reaper were sitting in a trailer at Creech Air Force Base, in the middle of the Nevada desert. The drone was flying well beneath the Hawk, at a little over ten thousand feet, and had just completed a run over the town for the second time after its bombs had destroyed the house where the hostages had been held. The pilot was responsible for deploying the Reaper's weapons, and he had done so reluctantly. There were Americans in that building. His only solace had been the certainty that he had given the poor bastards a swifter end than the one that would have awaited them otherwise.

The news that most of them had somehow managed to escape had filled him with relief.

The Reaper team had followed the Hawk's coordinates, and now they had a visual on the three vehicles that were running out of town.

The operator of the Hawk opened the channel. "Sentinel to Hammer. Are you seeing this?"

"Copy that, Sentinel," said the sensor operator. "Three possible targets, designated targets one through three. I am eyes on the first vehicle."

The woman stared at the feed from the Reaper's high-powered cameras, but it was too dark to make out any detail.

"Target one appears to be driven by one individual. Targets two and three appear to be armed pickup trucks. There are 12.7mm machine guns mounted in the flat beds, multiple passengers, all appear armed. Definitely hostile."

"Copy that, Hammer. Sentinel is going to try and get a better look."

The Mission Intelligence Controller was in the booth behind them. "Confirm weapons load-out," she said.

The pilot checked his screen. "I've got four missiles."

"Copy that."

The sensor operator relayed what she could see. "Target one is the lead vehicle. White sedan. It is three hundred and fifty feet ahead of Target two. Target two is a black pickup. Target three is a red pickup, thirty feet behind target two."

Mission Control was aboard the *Tortuga*. "This is Mission Control to Sentinel. What have you got on the lead car?"

"Sentinel to Mission Control. Stand by."

The Reaper pilot slipped his finger up his joystick to rest on the red launch trigger. "Permission to engage hostiles."

The MIC toggled her radio. "Creech to Mission Control," she said. "Permission to engage?"

⌣

Michael Pope was in the *Tortuga's* mission control room. There were four screens hung from the wall, and each showed a different feed. One each from the Reaper and the Hawk and two from the satellites. He squinted at the Hawk's feed, but the picture was grainy and disfigured by artefacts. He couldn't make the details out.

"I can't see a bloody thing," Pope growled at no one in particular. "The pilot needs to focus."

Lieutenant Commander McMahon gripped the edge of the table.

Neither he nor Pope could do any more than they were doing.

But if Beatrix was in any of those cars, then she was quickly running out of time.

The blinding flashes from the JDAMs had been visible from the ship and had heralded a bitter reaction from the crew. The terrorists might have been taken out, but the mission was still a failure. The sudden appearance of the hostages, with no time to spare, had rejuvenated the mood. Pope had explained what must have happened in the house. He said that their liberation could only have been Rose's doing, and a short radio message from the Mark V confirmed it: Captain Thomas said that they had been rescued by a blonde-haired woman. Pope had appealed to McMahon to send one of the boats back for her, but McMahon had turned him down. Pope wasn't surprised. The beach was hot, and there was no way that the SEALs could wait for her. Besides, Captain Thomas had also reported that he had watched her run back into Barawe.

If only he could have told her that he was going to be here, aboard the ship she would have been taken to, perhaps she would have made a different decision.

He cursed Stone afresh.

White tracer suddenly streaked across all four screens.

"What are they doing?" McMahon said.

The comms link that included all the participants in the raid was audible through the control room's speakers, and the Reaper's sensor operator cursed. "Target two is firing on target one. Shit, target three is firing, too. Repeat, target one is being fired at. The white sedan appears to be running from targets two and three."

At that precise moment the sedan swerved off the road. It went sideways, slewing to a stop. The passenger side door opened, and a figure got out and huddled down in the inadequate cover offered by the car's wing.

The driver looked up at the sky.

The Global Hawk's infrared cameras got a better view of the driver. It was dark, the view was brief and only partially clear, but Pope knew it was Beatrix.

"That's her," Pope said quickly.

McMahon spoke into the mic. "Roger, Hammer, this is Mission Control. Intent is to destroy targets two and three and their personnel. Weapons free, Hammer. Weapons free."

"Copy that," the Reaper pilot said. "Spinning up weapon on target three. Launch checklist. MTS autotrack?"

"Established," replied the sensor operator.

"Laser?"

"Armed."

"Fire the laser."

"Lasing."

"We're within range and we have a lock. Three, two, one, *rifle*."

Pope paused, watching the screen.

"Three, two, one, *impact*."

⌣

Beatrix pressed herself against the punctured wing of the car. A volley of rounds had pierced the metal and shredded the front tyres. The car had spun out of control, and it had been all she could do to prevent it from rolling over as it left the road.

It was a false victory.

She was stranded now, with nowhere to run, and the Technicals were racing towards her.

She touched her hand to her face. Her fingertips came back stained with blood.

The steady whining in her ears was worse.

She braced for the strafing that she knew was about to come. She had failed. She had only avenged herself on two of them. All she could hope for was that they would spare her daughter.

She reached into the car. The MP-5 had fallen into the footwell. She collected it.

No sense in delaying the inevitable.

The Technicals were slowing.

They stopped, twenty feet away. Cautious.

She had the MP-5 out of sight, below the hood. If she was going to go out, she would take as many of them with her as she could.

She stood.

She raised the submachine gun and fired, a tight burst that rattled into the bodywork of the nearest pickup.

The machine gun roared back at her, an elephant as to an ant.

Something glinted overhead.

She saw a streak of light flash down from the sky.

Fuck.

Beatrix dropped to her knees, wrapped her arms over her head and prayed.

There was a terrific eruption.

The explosion was close enough to the back of the Lada to lift it from its rear wheels. It crashed back down hard enough to shatter the axle.

A second later, the flaming remains of the first pickup crashed to earth, upside down, fifteen feet from where it had been standing. A wheel crashed against the roof of the wrecked Lada and bounced away into the desert. Fragments of metal pitter-pattered onto the dirt around her.

Beatrix crouched down in the shelter of the Lada and then risked a glance over the hood.

The second Technical had been too close and had been flipped onto its side by the brutal energy of the explosion. Its wheels continued to spin, and its engine howled, impotent now. The machine gun had snapped from its mount and had been scattered to the side. The men in the back of the pickup had been flung away by the impact of the crash. Some of them were unmoving. Others were groggily pushing themselves to their hands and knees.

The driver's side door was pressed against the ground. A leg kicked through the passenger window and the driver hauled himself out.

She heard a weak voice. *"Sa'adni!"*—*"Help me."*

The driver was still trying to drag himself away from the shattered cab when the second Hellfire missile streaked down from the heavens.

Incoming.

Beatrix covered her head again as the explosion cast reds and oranges across the brightening sky.

Chapter Twenty-Eight

The ziggurat that housed the Secret Intelligence Service had been completed in 1994, the same year that MI6 had been officially acknowledged for the first time. It was a vast building, almost 300,000 square feet, and was constructed in bombproof, man-made, ochre granite. Ten floors rose step by step into the London skyline, including the executive suite on the top floor, where Benjamin Stone had his offices. There were another six below ground, too, housing command centres, laboratories and a workshop. Tourists gaped at it from the river boats that plied the Thames, their credulous interest fanned by cockney geezers who made all the obvious links to James Bond and Le Carré. They said it was influenced by ancient Persian architecture and that the people who worked there referred to it as "Babylon-on-Thames."

Pope had taken a circuitous route along the river. He walked slowly, allowing his thoughts to flash across the last couple of days and the assessment he would be asked to deliver. He had been helicoptered from the *Tortuga* to Dadaab and had flown back from there to RAF Northolt, touching down twelve hours ago. He had slept on the flight, but it had been fitful and unsatisfying, even with the comfort of the Gulfstream. The government car had picked him up and delivered him back to the anonymous offices where Group Fifteen did their business.

He turned away from the river and turned again onto the Albert Embankment, following the pavement at the edge of the building, watching the fountains bubbling behind an iron fence and before the bombproof walls. People who worked here called their employer The Firm. The only department more secretive than this was the one that Pope commanded. That didn't make him feel any better as he turned in and approached the wide steel doors with the armed guards behind them and the phalanx of CCTV cameras swivelling overhead. This was the organisation that John Milton had defied, and it had chased him to the ends of the earth.

Police armed with Heckler & Koch submachine guns watched new arrivals with wary interest. Pope lined up for his turn to pass through a row of six time-locked security doors, stacked like the eggs of a giant insect. The queue shuffled forward. When it was Pope's turn to enter, he stepped into one of the booths, swiped his security card and stooped down to the iris scanner. The laser flashed across his eye, left to right and then right to left, and satisfied, the security program opened the inner door for him. He stepped forward into the narrow capsule; the outer door closed behind him, the sensor in the floor confirmed that he was the only occupant, and the inner door slid open.

The inner lobby reminded Pope of the interior of a flashy, but soulless, hotel. Soft fluorescent light from recessed sconces in the vaulted ceiling sparkled on an ivory marble floor. The walls were slate and matt grey. Two giant columns dominated the hall, each containing banks of elevators. Leather benches were furnished around the circumference of the columns, and natural light filtered down from an atrium that opened through a tall light well to the iron sky above.

Pope reached the desk.

"Your name, sir?"

"Captain Michael Pope."

The man ran his finger down the monitor in front of him, found Pope's name and printed out a visitor's pass. He attached it to a lanyard and handed it to him.

"Take the lift to the eighth floor, sir. An aide will be waiting for you there."

Pope was met in the elevator lobby by an aide he recognised from a previous visit.

"Good afternoon, sir," the man said.

"Good afternoon."

"Sir Benjamin is waiting for you."

Pope followed the aide. The hive of corridors was unmarked and the doors labelled with seemingly meaningless acronyms. The bare workspaces were all open plan, the space carved into anonymous cubicles, the officers who inhabited each of them working at their screens with urgent concentration. They processed information, collated files, planned operations, liaised with foreign intelligence networks and provided support to the men and women in the field, including the agents under Pope's command. They continued on, passing server rooms shielded to prevent eavesdropping (Pope had heard that some of them, the particularly important ones, were encased within a foot of lead) and reached a second, secure lobby with just a single elevator. They entered the waiting car and ascended the remaining distance to the executive floor.

The intercom buzzed discreetly, the doors opened and Pope followed the aide out into the vestibule beyond.

It was quiet up here. Pope turned left out of the doors and padded behind the man, across deeply piled carpet, all the way to the chrome and brushed-glass door that led to the offices of Sir Benjamin Stone and his staff.

The aide opened the door and showed Pope through to the last room on the right.

When Pope came in through the door, Stone was sitting at his wide desk, speaking to someone with the aid of a Bluetooth headset that seemed awkward and out of place on his head. He made an impatient gesture towards the chair on the other side of the desk, and Pope walked over and sat down. The conversation seemed important. Pope caught references to the situation in Somalia, and Stone raised his hand and extended two fingers to indicate how long he thought it would last before it was finished.

Pope smiled patiently and looked around. The room was furnished in the same style as the entrance on the ground floor, with the expensive minimalism of a high-end business hotel. The furniture was Scandinavian, brusquely utilitarian, and there was little concession to personality or to the humanity of its occupant. The windows had a green tint and were triple-glazed to protect against laser and radio frequency flooding.

He shifted in his chair and looked down at his hands, idly rubbing the calloused skin. He looked back up at C., who took a pipe from his desk and filled the bowl with tobacco from a pouch in his pocket. He tamped the bowl down, struck a match and lit it. Of course, smoking was not permitted inside the building, but there were rules and then there were rules, and some of them were ignored, depending upon who was involved.

Stone finished the call with an exasperated "Thank God for that." He leaned back in his chair. "Sorry about that, Pope. Our friends in America are congratulating themselves on a job well done. I'm expected to pat them on the back and tell them how impressed we all are. I suppose we can allow them their moment."

"How many people know about what happened?"

"The operational people. But they're all pretending she wasn't there."

"The SEALs were on their way home when she brought the hostages out."

"Yes, true, but like I said, we'll let them think otherwise if it keeps them sweet, eh? It's not as if she's an official asset, and we don't want to be claiming credit for someone who burst into the room and executed two of the hostages. We can't go claiming the credit for that, can we?" He screwed up his eyes without humour.

"No, sir. We certainly can't."

"There's deniable, and then there's Ms Rose. That's something else entirely." Stone wrestled the headset off his head and tossed it onto the empty glass desk in front of him. "Foolish things," he said.

There was silence for a moment. Pope glanced out of the window as a helicopter followed the line of the river, its engine silenced by the triple glazing. He looked back at C. and searched his broad, wrinkled face for any clue that might have explained why he had wanted to see him in person.

"Look, Pope," C. said after a pause, jabbing the pipe in his direction. "I know you have a lot on your plate with rebuilding the Group after that nonsense in Russia, but I wanted to tell you that our mutual friend's success has been passed up the chain right to the top. And I mean *right* to the top. The foreign secretary and the prime minister have both been briefed on what she's done and what she's trying to do. The whole situation with Control was a monumental fuck-up. I can't emphasise that enough. If he was to be turned by one of our enemies, by one of our friends, even, it would make Philby and his chums look like a teddy bears' picnic. He knows enough to bring down the government. And that's not an overestimation."

"No, sir. I don't believe that it is."

"Everyone is in agreement that we are handling it the correct way. We don't know where he is. Until we do, we will follow every lead we can that might bring us closer to him. It might be that the other four that Rose is after can shed some light on where he's gone to ground. I'm assuming she is the persuasive type?"

"Yes, sir. She is."

"Maybe she can work through them and end up with him."

"So we continue to support her?"

"We do. Until I say otherwise, she's our best hope at putting this whole sorry mess to bed."

"Very good, sir."

He drew down on the pipe. "You're the cut-out on this, Pope. If it goes wrong, it'll be your neck on the block. I know that's unfair, but that's how it's going to have to be."

"I understand, sir. That's the job."

"That *is* the job. Good man."

Stone took a sheaf of paper from the tray on his desk and flipped it over to him.

"Might have something on the next chap on Rose's list."

"Duffy?"

He nodded. "Look it over. It's up to you how you give it to her."

The conversation was at an end. He got up and half-turned towards the door.

"How good is she, Pope?"

"Rose?" He paused. "She's good, sir. Very good. I know one thing for sure: I wouldn't want to be the one she was coming after."

Chapter Twenty-Nine

The medina was as crazed and chaotic as it ever was as Beatrix Rose stepped out of the taxi. They were on Dar El Bacha, and the driver was starting to grumble that he had taken her as far as he could. The traffic, he said; the people. Beatrix didn't mind. She was happy to walk. She paid him his fare and set off on the last leg of her journey.

It had been a difficult exfiltration. The Lada had been wrecked, and she had abandoned it. She had hiked onwards for five hours until she had flagged down a truck heading south. It was another smuggler, and she had been able to pay him for a lift in the back of a truck that was using the *panyos* to smuggle oranges and lemons past the border patrol.

He had dropped her just across the line, and after a three-hour walk to the Garissa Road, she had managed to flag down a UN bus loaded with refugees for a ride into the camp at Dadaab. She had collected her Land Cruiser from where she had parked it and had driven for eight hours on the battered old route A3 to Nairobi.

From there, it had been an Emirates flight from Nairobi to Dubai, a connecting flight to Casablanca and then a final connection with Royal Air Maroc to Marrakech. She had been travelling for another twenty-four hours by the time she had disembarked from the taxi, and she was dog tired. She had taken more ibuprofen than was safe, but there had been no easy way to get morphine, and she had needed something to deaden the pain. And what did it matter in the grand scheme of things? Her liver, after all, was the least of her worries.

She followed the maze of ever-narrowing passageways until she reached the thick wooden door of "La Villa des Orangers."

She banged on it.

Mohammed opened up after a few seconds, his face morphing from one of happy surprise to one of concern. "Madam Beatrix," he said, "my heart is glad to see you."

"Hello Mohammed," she said.

"Forgive me, but you look dreadful."

"I could sleep for a week," she said, although she thought, as she said it, that it was not true.

Physically, she could.

But practically?

There was no time for a prolonged recovery.

She had to keep moving.

Perpetual motion.

Like a shark.

He helped her inside.

"How's Isabella?" she asked him.

"You should see for yourself," he said.

"Where is she?"

"On the range."

* * *

She heard the silenced pistol as she crossed the courtyard. Her daughter was at one end of the range, as far as she could get from the target on the opposite wall. The distance from wall to wall was fifteen metres. That was plenty for the purposes of sharpening up her aim. She wouldn't be using her secondary weapon for a target farther away than that, anyway. That was why you carried a long gun. Beatrix intended to introduce that into her training when she was satisfied that Bella had mastered a pistol. After that, if they had time, there would be knives and grenades, and then, if they were lucky, tradecraft.

Isabella took aim and squeezed off each shot at an interval of a second, just as she had been taught.

Beatrix waited until the girl saw her.

"Mummy!" she said.

She hugged her daughter to her, forgetting the pain in her bones in the warmth of her child's embrace.

"That looked pretty good."

Beatrix watched as Isabella ran to the bottom of the range, tore out the perforated target and brought it back.

The target was an outline of a man with a Kalashnikov. Isabella had put all ten rounds inside the cartoon head.

"Can't do much better than that."

"I've practised every day, like you said."

"Good girl."

"I want to try a full auto. Can I?"

"Soon. I'm going to stock up. I'll get something you'll be able to manage."

Another wave of fatigue washed over her, and she had to brace a hand on the windowsill to maintain her balance.

"Are you alright?"

"Just tired, darling. It was a long trip."

Isabella pointed up to Beatrix's head. "What happened to your hair?"

Beatrix raised her hand to her head and felt the burnt ends prickle across her palm. "There was a little explosion. I was a bit closer to it than I would have liked."

"And your face?"

She meant the tens of tiny cuts from the glass shards that had showered over her after the windshield was blown out.

"Scratches."

"So you're alright?"

"Yes," she said, smiling. "I'm fine. No damage done."

"How did it go?"

"It went well."

"You got him?"

"I did."

"Two down."

"That's right. And four to go."

"I'm pleased you're home, Mummy."

"I'm pleased too, sweetheart."

Beatrix took the Glock and ejected the dry magazine. She handed it to her daughter.

"You know why I want you to practise as much as you can, don't you?"

"You want me to be good."

"Why?"

"Because they're coming."

"That's right. And because they know I'm coming. And they're going to do everything they can to stop me."

"And we can't hide from them."

"No, we can't. They'd find us eventually."

"So we've got to be prepared."

"I want you to practise and practise and practise, so that when someone comes through that door with a gun or a knife, you won't be scared when you have to pull a gun and put a nine-millimetre round right through his eye."

"Wouldn't be scared now," Isabella said, thumbing another ten rounds into the magazine.

"No, baby-doll," Beatrix said. "I don't think you would."

She replaced the target with a fresh one and stepped to the side as her daughter raised the suppressed Glock and fired off another round.

They *were* coming.

She knew it.

But she was coming, too.

Beatrix Rose's story continues in
BLOOD MOON RISING.
Here's an extract from the first chapter.

It was three in the morning when Beatrix Rose finally reached the Wiltshire village where Lydia Chisholm had her house. She had been following her for two hours, all the way south from London. She turned the stolen Kawasaki off the A road, passed a cute village pub and then turned sharply behind it and followed a gentle rise to a series of even prettier houses. Beatrix had extinguished the headlamp five minutes earlier, and now she killed the engine, freewheeling to a stop. She flicked out the kickstand and rested the bike on it carefully. Chisholm's top-of-the-range BMW drove on and parked next to a dark blue Audi A3. Beatrix jogged along the road, keeping close to the thick verge of hawthorn, her rucksack bouncing up and down on her back.

Chisholm and her husband got out, locked the door and climbed the steps from the road to the front door. Chisholm went first, opening the door and stepping inside. Her husband followed. A hall light flicked on.

Beatrix edged closer to the house. Some of the nearby dwellings were thatched, and all of them looked expensive. The mainline station was a ten-minute drive away, and London was ninety minutes by train from there. It was at the edge of a reasonable distance to consider commuting, and Beatrix guessed that the people who did travel in from the village were more likely to be senior staff who had the latitude to work from home. That supposition was borne out by the cars that were parked along the edge of the road: Range Rovers, Porsches, Jaguars, more BMWs. The houses had big extensions, manicured gardens, swimming pools. There was money here, and influence, too. But she had known that already.

Chisholm and her husband had been in town all day. Chisholm had been to a meeting of the board of private security contractors that she had established after leaving Group Fifteen. Manage Risk was a serious concern, with offices around the world, and it counted among its senior employees one of Chisholm's old colleagues in the Group, Joshua Joyce. Beatrix had been in Somalia last week, where she had reacquainted herself with Joyce. He had been assigned as security on a freighter that had been captured by al-Shabaab off the coast. Beatrix had infiltrated the country and the town in which the terrorists had made their stronghold.

Joyce was an ex-employee now.

She had struck his name from her Kill List.

Beatrix had returned home to Morocco to find excellent news waiting for her. Michael Pope, the new Control of Group Fifteen, had provided her with the news that they had located Chisholm, too. Beatrix had immediately boarded a flight from Marrakech to Heathrow. She had followed Chisholm for two days and constructed the plan that was now drawing to its conclusion.

Chisholm's house was a large square building with broad windows on both sides of the porch, four or five windows on the first floor and a dormer on top. It looked as if it was in the middle of a refurbishment program. The stonework had been repointed, and the lime render on the exterior walls was fresh. There was an alarm box beneath the eaves and a satellite dish positioned discreetly away from public view. There was a broad lawn to the right of the house, with what looked like a tennis court behind it and an ornamental garden to the left. The land sloped up steeply behind the property, with the deeper darkness of a copse of tall fir and oak providing a border to that side.

Beatrix waited until the downstairs light was switched off and then moved forward. A stone wall separated the property from the road, and she slipped between it and the BMW, dropping down to her belly and slithering forward. The car was still warm, the engine ticking as the temperature bled away in the coolness of the night. She removed the rucksack and opened it, taking out three pounds of Semtex and a disposable mobile phone that she had purchased earlier that day. The phone was wrapped around the detonator with gaffer tape, and that, in turn, was wrapped around the plastique. She checked that the wire connecting the phone to the detonator was still in place, peeled away the adhesive backing and pressed the bomb to the underside of the car, right below the fuel tank.

She had a few hours to wait.

She made her way back to her motorbike and hid it in a nearby lane, beneath a railway bridge that boomed and shook as a late night goods train rumbled over it. She clambered over a nearby fence and negotiated a paddock and then a pig field until she had found her way to the large garden at the back of Chisholm's house. There was a tumbledown shed next to the vegetable patch, and it offered a decent view of the house, the BMW and the road for twenty yards on either side. It was perfect.

Beatrix took out her night vision binoculars, zipped up her leather jacket and settled down to wait.

Acknowledgements

I am indebted to the following for their help, all above and beyond the call of duty: Lucy Dawson, for her early edits and direction; Martha Hayes, for masterful and thoughtful editing; and Detective Lieutenant (Ret'd) Edward L. Dvorak, Los Angeles County Sheriff's Department, and Joe D. Gillespie, for their advice on weapons and military matters.

I'd like to thank the Apub team, including Emilie Marneu and Jennifer McIntyre.

The following members of Team Milton were also invaluable: Lee Robertson, Nigel Foster, Frank Wells, Gary Pugsley, Brian Ellis, Bob, Mel Murray, Phil Powell, Charlie, Matt Ballard, Edward Short, Desiree Brown, Don Lehman, Barry Franklin, Corne van der Merwe, Dawn Taybron, Paul Quish, Carl Hinds, Chuck Harkins, Don, Mike Wright, Julian Annells, Charles Rolfe, Michael Conway, Grant Brown, Rick Lowe, Randall Masteller and Chris Orrick.

Want to Get the Mark Dawson Starter Library?

Building a relationship with my readers is the very best thing about writing. I occasionally send newsletters with details on new releases, special offers and other bits of news relating to the John Milton, Beatrix Rose and Soho Noir series. And if you sign up to my no-spam mailing list, I'll send you all this free stuff:

1. A copy of my bestseller *The Cleaner*.
2. A copy of the John Milton introductory novella, *1000 Yards*.
3. A copy of my bestseller *The Black Mile*.
4. A copy of the introductory Soho Noir Novella, *Gaslight*.
5. A copy of the highly classified background check on John Milton before he was admitted to Group 15. Exclusive to my mailing list—you can't get this anywhere else.

You can get the novels, the novellas, the background check and the short story for free, by signing up at http://eepurl.com/UsJ3f.

About the Author

Mark Dawson has worked as a lawyer and in the London film industry.

He has written three series: John Milton features a disgruntled government hit man trying to right wrongs in order to make amends for the things he's done; Beatrix Rose traces the headlong fight for justice of a wronged mother and trained assassin; and Soho Noir is set in the West End of London between 1940 and 1970. Mark lives in Wiltshire, in the UK, with his family.

You can find him at www.markjdawson.com, www.facebook .com/markdawsonauthor and on Twitter at @pbackwriter.

Printed in Great Britain
by Amazon.co.uk, Ltd.,
Marston Gate.